Praise for A De

T0161721

'Paolo Maurensi~ .... engaging literary fable on narcissism and vainglory, and also on our inextinguishable thirst for stories'
Q Libri

'In addition to the beauty of the plot of *A Devil Comes to Town*, one appreciates the refinement with which Maurensig tackles strong and intimate themes such as narcissism, self-awareness, and the Sartrean archetype of "hell is other people"'
EsteticaMente

'Paolo Maurensig skillfully mixes bizarre narrative with great truths about the human soul'
GraphoMania

'A diabolical game that convinces from start to finish. With this short novel, Maurensig offers us an apologue on the literary world that speaks of a country in which everyone writes, and where to breathe the air becomes hellish. The author of *The Lüneburg Variation* pulls the reader into a plot so intriguing and absorbing that it almost feels like reading a thriller'
Liberidiscrivere

'Maurensig has created a gripping short novel that is critical about the realities of publishing, a hybrid of at least two genres, highly imaginative, and involving even beyond the final page'
Critica Letteraria

'Biblical, oblique, and lying somewhere between thriller, fantasy, and legend, the new novel by Paolo Maurensig, *A Devil Comes to Town*, is a disturbing reflection in narrative form concerning the darker side of writing'
Il Giornale

'A cultured and refined divertissement—with enjoyable retro references to late-romantic gothic literature, to the fantasy of Von Chamisso, to Hoffmann, and to Schnitzler's later works—this book is also a pungent and very topical apologue'
Cronache Letterarie

'Intelligently constructed and written in an elegant and refined style, this is a gem for even the most formidable readers; a fantastic little book that will keep you entertained for several wonderful hours over the weekend. Don't miss it!'
Passione per Libri

'*A Devil Comes to Town* blew my mind—think Yorgos Lanthimos directing *The Master and Margarita*. It's a bizarre slice of Alpine magic realism that deserves to be everywhere'
The Observer

PAOLO MAURENSIG was born in Gorizo, and lives in Udine, Italy. Now a bestselling author, he debuted in 1993 with *The Lüneburg Variation*, which has sold over a million copies worldwide and been translated into 38 languages. His novels include *Canone Inverso*, *The Guardian of Dreams*, and *The Archangel of Chess*. For his novel *Theory of Shadows*, published by FSG in the US in 2018, he won the Bagutta Prize. *A Devil Comes to Town* is his latest novel.

ANNE MILANO APPEL has translated works by Claudio Magris, Paolo Giordano, Paolo Maurensig, Giuseppe Catozzella, Primo Levi, Roberto Saviano, and many others. Her awards include the Italian Prose in Translation Award (2015), the John Florio Prize for Italian Translation (2013), and the Northern California Book Award for Translation (2014 and 2013).

A Devil Comes to Town

Published in the USA in 2019 by World Editions LLC, New York
Published in the UK in 2019 by World Editions Ltd., London

World Editions
New York/London/Amsterdam

Copyright © Paolo Maurensig, 2018
English translation copyright © Anne Milano Appel, 2019
Cover image © Charles Fréger
Author's portrait © Graziano Arici / agefotostock.com

Printed by Sheridan, Chelsea, MI, USA

This book is a work of fiction. Any resemblance to actual persons,
living or dead, or actual events is purely coincidental.

Library of Congress Cataloging in Publication Data is available
ISBN 978-1-64286-013-9
First published as *Il diavolo nel cassetto* in Italy in 2018 by Einaudi

All rights reserved. No part of this publication may be reproduced,
stored in or introduced into a retrieval system, or transmitted, in any
form, or by any means (electronic, mechanical, photocopying, record-
ing or otherwise) without the prior written permission of the publisher.

Twitter: @WorldEdBooks
Facebook: WorldEditionsInternationalPublishing
www.worldeditions.org

Book Club Discussion Guides are available on our website.

Paolo Maurensig

A Devil Comes to Town

Translated from the Italian
by Anne Milano Appel

WORLD EDITIONS
New York, London, Amsterdam

What can prompt us to approach the difficult task of re-examining the many useless items that we've accumulated over the years and never found the courage to discard? An upcoming move maybe, or—as in my case—the need to clear out a room, till now a repository for worthless junk, so it could be put to different use. I can't think of any other reason. Before parting with an object, we think twice about it, and most of the time we choose to keep it, convincing ourselves that it might be useful again in the future. Meanwhile things pile up until we are forced to make a clean sweep. Then we begin a journey back in memory: we browse through our past, we pause to gaze at old photos, to reread letters that we don't remember having received, books with dedications, manuscripts ... and I had stacks and stacks of those: since the publication of a fortuitous novel had afforded me a certain renown, I had become a pole of attraction for aspiring writers. Their manuscripts started coming with impressive regularity, the authors all requesting that I not only read them but give them my *authoritative* opinion, and possibly introduce them to some publisher, perhaps with the addition of a preface written in my hand. At the beginning I would take the trouble to read the texts through to the end, but I quickly realized that I would never be able to keep up, and that I would be spending most of my time on works of little or no interest. Getting rid of them, however, isn't so easy: if it already pains me to have to part with an object, no matter how useless it may be, there is a certain regard for the author that each time stops me from disposing of the manuscripts. Consequently, I wanted to make sure I hadn't made any error of assessment before sending them to be pulped. As I sat there flipping through one manuscript after another, I came across a large manila envelope, still sealed, amply covered by a mosaic of stamps from the Helvetic Confederation. I tore open the flap and found myself holding a text of roughly a hundred typed pages. There was no letter attached, nor was there a sender's name, or a return address to be traced. Evidently the author wanted to remain anonymous. Or perhaps he meant to reveal himself in the course of the reading.

The title was: *The Devil in the Drawer*, and it began like this:

I tremble at the mere thought of having set this story on paper. For a long time I held it inside me, but in the end I had to unburden myself from a weight that threatened to compromise my mental equilibrium. Because it is certainly a story leading to the brink of madness. Yet I listened to it through to the end, without ever doubting the words of that man. All the more so because he was a priest.

I can understand that to the reader's eyes all this has the appearance of a narrative device; literature is full of manuscripts, diaries, letters, and memos found in the most unexpected places and in the most unforeseen ways. But when you think about it, all stories begin by being drafted or printed on paper; everything we read begins with a ream of sheets, or rather, a manuscript, one of the many that pile up on a publisher's desk or that of whoever is responsible for reading them for him. There was nothing extraordinary, therefore, in the discovery of this one: that bundle of pages was in the right place, only it had escaped my attention. The only thing strange about it was the anonymity.

The incipit seemed promising. And so, sitting right smack in the middle of all kinds of tattered texts, leaving my clean-up work half finished, I went on reading.

Though the author avoids revealing his name, he nevertheless sets the scene for the beginning of his story by specifying the date and location. It all goes back to September 1991, during a brief stay in Switzerland, specifically in Küsnacht, a small town that overlooks Lake Zurich, where our author traveled to attend a conference on psychoanalysis.

I was there as a consultant for a small publishing house that wanted to include in its catalog a series dedicated to this fascinating as well as controversial subject. Put that way, one might think that I played an important role. In reality, the publishing house belonged to my uncle who, already the owner of a typography shop, after having printed thousands of volumes on behalf of third parties, had been seized by the sudden ambition to become a publisher himself, hiring me more out of familial obligation than for any recognized merits.

A few words to tell us something about himself. He immediately reveals his condition as an orphan: his mother died giving birth to him, his father passed away a few years later, the victim of an accident on the job, and he himself was raised by his paternal uncle. We also discover that he is devoured by a passion for writing, and thanks to these disclosures, we are able to attribute an age to him: rather young, one would say, around twenty-five or thirty. Speaking in the first person, the author has no need to reveal his name, but to avoid unnecessary circumlocutions, I will assign him one. I will call him Friedrich: a name that I feel suggests a pale, blondish, aspiring writer rambling through the valleys of Switzerland.

Speaking of his uncle, Friedrich says and I quote:

Books were the only thing we had in common: he aspired to publish them, I to write them. In fact, I found myself in that blessed larval state that we all pass through as soon as we discover (or delude ourselves) that we are called to one of the arts. For a certain time, I had been the errand boy at a local newspaper in exchange for a wage that was barely enough for cigarettes. I edited the obituary page and occasionally minor news briefs. I had published a short story or two in that paper, just to fill up the page. If there was a scarcity of news and some free space still remaining, the editor-in-chief would then have me dash off a little narrative no longer than 700 words. So, I had never written anything that went beyond the short story, never published except on the pages of that provincial newspaper, but deep within me I nurtured a dream; I endured that fallow period waiting for a seed sown in the ground to sprout, until before long it might reach the size of a lush, fruit-bearing plant.

When I was later hired by my uncle in the publishing house,

with the job of reading manuscripts and correcting page proofs, I felt like I had taken a step forward. I lived surrounded by books, breathing in the scent of printers' ink that to me was as intoxicating as a drug. I assumed the airs of a writer, with a notebook and pencil always in my pocket, ready when needed. I observed people, trying to read in each of them his individual story ... and yet I doubted that anyone would ever think of telling it to me someday. In any case, I had a permanent job in a publishing house and, though it was poorly compensated, I held on tightly to it. And this was my first important out-of-town mission. My uncle had assigned me this task thanks to my command of the German language—though it has little similarity to the local parlance.

Carl Gustav Jung had lived and died in Küsnacht, and that year, on the occasion of the thirtieth anniversary of his death, there was a three-day conference that involved experts from all over the world. Listening to the speakers, famous in their circles but to me completely unknown, I might perhaps come upon some text to publish, one not too pretentious, thereby inaugurating the new editorial series. Possibly I would not find anything of interest, and if that were the case—so be it!—I would enjoy a brief vacation at the company's expense.

I had not thought about booking a hotel, so I had to settle for staying at the Gasthof Adler, a clean, quiet inn, somewhat out of the way. An ideal place to write, I immediately thought—at that time I assessed everything with the eye of an ambitious writer. The inn was a few kilometers from the town center, where the conference was being held in a municipal auditorium. There was a postbus that came by every hour, but even on foot it wasn't a very long walk, and if you wanted to shorten it, you could take a path that cut through a dense fir wood. The weather was beautiful, the lakeside air invigorated the lungs, and in the sunlight the palettes of the rosebushes that adorned every house—from the villas to the more modest dwellings—were an enchantment for the eyes. So, that morning I had decided to go on foot. I could not yet know that something would soon cloud the idyllic image that I had formed of the place. It was an encounter that took place under peculiar circumstances. I was walking toward town along the path that went through the woods, when all of a sudden I heard a scuffling coming from the underbrush. I stopped, curious. My first thought was that some frightened animal—perhaps a deer—would suddenly dash out in front of me. Instead, I soon saw that it was a man whose body was so enormous that he appeared misshapen. Wearing a split leather smock, he was stumbling through the trees holding a plastic bucket filled with a reddish pulp and flinging handfuls of it on the ground. When he became aware of my presence, he looked up at me: the receding chin and drooping lower lip made me think of a mentally retarded person who had been assigned a task that no one else would want to do. As soon as he saw me, the man waved his arm as if warning me of some danger. What was he trying to tell me with that gesture? I continued along the path gripped by a growing sense of unease, as if I had trespassed on private property. I wanted nothing more than to get away from that place as soon as possible and reach the village. I must have walked a few hundred meters, when I heard the hurried step of someone behind me who was going in my direction. For a moment I thought it was the man I had just seen going through the woods, but the pace was too agile and swift for a person of his girth. I kept going straight and only turned around at the last moment, when the stranger was about to catch up to me. I immediately felt a sense of relief when I saw that it was a priest. A Catholic priest: complete with cassock and wide-brimmed saturn. Small and somewhat bent—just as I had always pictured Father Brown—, he came alongside me with a quick step and, after greeting me briefly, promptly warned me. "Watch out for the foxes," he said excitedly, "don't let them come near you: there's an epidemic of wild rabies going around." Having said that, he went on his way, quickly leaving me behind before disappearing around the first curve of the winding path. He seemed in such a hurry—as if the devil were literally on his heels—that it made me fearful of imminent danger. I was at the point where the woods grew more dense and the tops of the taller firs obscured the pale disk of the sun. It may have been suggestion caused by that strange warning, but I suddenly felt as if I was about to have a panic attack. I picked up a sturdy dead branch, ready to defend myself if needed, and started running in a vain attempt to reach the priest who, with his sprinter's pace, had by then vanished. Gradually, however, as the first houses and the dazzling glimmer of the lake appeared through the firs, I regained my control.

Friedrich, therefore, reaches the village, where everyday life unfolds in an orderly and peaceful manner. In the midst of all that normalcy, he smiles at the thought of having been the victim of irrational fear. What has just happened to him seems almost unreal. Soon enough he convinces himself that it was just a trick of the imagination. He enters the conference hall and takes a seat in one of the few chairs still free. For a few minutes he absently follows the talk already underway: a bombastic excursus on Jung's life. Then, among the numerous bearded professors with their flowing white manes—some with an unlit pipe between their teeth—, he spots the small Catholic priest he'd just met in the woods, sitting a dozen or so rows further up. He soon finds out that the cleric is one of the speakers. When the talk in progress ends, in fact, the priest takes his turn at the lectern. Friedrich consults the program he has in his pocket. It is the last talk of the morning, and will end at noon. At that precise moment the town hall clock strikes ten, and with Swiss punctuality the floor passes to Father Cornelius—that was the priest's name—whose talk is entitled: "The Devil As Transformist." So that explained all that hurrying, thinks Friedrich, evidently he was worried about being late for the conference: a failing that the audience members would have considered unforgivable.

The cleric addresses the problem of evil and its emissary with various digressions into the world of art and literature, in order to arrive at a particular point of view, namely, the notion of a devil incarnate who blends in among people and can play multiple roles, at times assuming the identity and appearance of apparently normal individuals, with whom we have daily personal relationships ... No sulfur fumes, therefore, but the ordinary quotidian. The priest's theory soon provokes divergent opinions. A theme so "secular," put forth in that shrine of the psyche in an almost disarming way by a little country priest, can't help but raise some sardonic comments, to the point that some leave the room protesting. To Friedrich, however, the topic seems rather original, and could very well constitute a book; moreover, the exposition is clear and the language is within everyone's reach, like that of a Sunday sermon. Friedrich listens to the priest eagerly, not missing a single word, and is more and more convinced that he has found what he was looking for. So he will not go back to his uncle empty-handed after all, and perhaps may even merit a fitting increase in pay. In his mind he can already see the priest's spoken words printed on paper, covering numerous pages that pile up on his desk to form a volume; he can even picture the cover. Meanwhile, time has flown by: the two hours scheduled for the talk have elapsed and with admirable synchrony, at the stroke of twelve, Father Cornelius concludes his talk, met by tepid applause. Friedrich's first impulse is to approach the priest, but he is swallowed up by a crowd that flocks toward the exit and is pushed out of the hall. Then, when the crowd has thinned out and he returns to the conference room, there is no longer any trace of the cleric.

Several pages follow in which Friedrich expresses his concerns to the reader. He fears, in fact, that he will not see the priest again, that once his talk was over, he may have left immediately. His attempts, at the conference's secretarial office, to find out where the cleric is staying are also hopeless: faced with the obdurate recalcitrance of the local dialect, his polished German seems to have become an incomprehensible foreign language. So for the entire afternoon Friedrich roams around the village in the hope of running into Father Cornelius, until toward evening he decides to return to the inn. He is tired and disappointed, and also famished. He knows that the Gasthof Adler's kitchen closes at a certain time, and after having skipped lunch, he doesn't feel like going to bed without supper as well. But when he gets back, a surprise awaits him.

As soon as I entered the dining room, I saw him sitting in a corner, the only guest in there, intent on eating his meal. After looking for him in vain all day, there he was, Father

Cornelius! It didn't seem real. Thinking about our encounter along the path leading to town, I should have imagined that he too was staying at the Gasthof Adler, since there were, in fact, no other hotels or inns nearby. This time I would not let him slip away. Judging by what was still on his plate, I estimated I had enough time to attempt a conversation. I sat down not too far away, but he did not seem to notice my presence; he was completely absorbed in his thoughts, and occasionally his lips moved as if he were speaking to himself. That evening, as the last arrival, I had to settle for a cold platter accompanied by a pint of beer; for the moment it was enough to appease my hunger, however, since my thoughts were wandering elsewhere. What was most urgent for me, in fact, was to find the right words to start a discourse. I was simply waiting for the right moment, which, however, never seemed to arrive. Both due to the presence of the waitress, who couldn't wait to be able to clear the table, and the fact that the priest was in a totally different world, it became increasingly difficult to attempt a first approach. Several times I'd cleared my throat to say something, perhaps to praise his lecture, or remind him of our brief encounter in the woods. It wouldn't have taken much, but each time something prevented me at the last moment. On the other hand, I didn't stop observing him for one instant. It may have been due to the poor lighting in the room and the dark wood-paneled walls, but compared to the brilliant speaker I had heard only a few hours earlier, I now seemed to have a different person before me: a weary, frowning man, oppressed by his thoughts. By now he had emptied his plate, and I could only count on the time it would take him to down the two gulps of beer that still remained in his glass; a sip or two, after which he might well get up and go, leaving me in the lurch. I had to make a move. Suddenly, however, sensing that he was being watched, the priest looked up at me. He stared at me for a few moments, then gave a slight smile, a sign that he had recognized me.

"I hope," he said, "that I did not alarm you too much this morning." And not giving me time to reply, he went on: "Did you know that every year hundreds of thousands of people throughout the world die because of this terrible disease? Naturally, this occurs in areas far removed from civilization: in certain villages in Africa or Asia, too far from a hospital that could ensure timely treatment. These poor people are destined for an atrocious end, atrocious for themselves and for their family members, who can do very little to alleviate their suffering."

I didn't know what to say, so I threw out a question:

"And did you have the chance to witness one of these patients on his death bed?"

"It's a sight that I would not wish anyone to see."

For a moment the priest lowered his eyes, as if regretting what had slipped out of his mouth. He surely thought that he had to justify such a statement: "Rabies, which the fox is recognized as the main carrier of, arouses an atavistic fear in us, since it not only leads to a horrible death, but is able to bring out from human nature what we have always tried to conceal: the irrepressible viciousness that lies hidden in all of us. What's more, the fox's cry is chilling enough to make the most courageous person's skin crawl. All this fuels popular superstition, which often associates the fox with the devil. And it's truly a pity that such a charming little creature is forced to bear such a grim reputation."

At that point the priest stopped short, as if realizing too late that he had been impolite to me: though I might seem like little more than a boy in his eyes, his having addressed me so abruptly did not fall within the rules of good manners.

He tried to make up for it then: he got up from his seat, came over to me, and after the proper introductions he asked permission to sit at my table. I gladly agreed, and was able to observe him more closely. It was difficult to attribute an age to him; his face seemed pallid, his expression brooding, and his short, reddish hair still bore the indentation mark left by the ecclesiastical saturn ...

"Are you here for the conference?" he asked.

With that question he made things easier for me, giving me the opportunity to brag a little.

"I'm a consultant for a publishing house," I said. "I'm here hoping to find a text to publish in our new series. In fact, I have to say that when I listened to your talk today I found it very interesting. Your literary references: Goethe, Mann, Hoffmann, symbolist painting ... At times though I had the impression that the things you left unsaid were more numerous than those you did say. It seemed to me that you were speaking about the devil as if he were a real existent being."

"In fact that is the case. Only I couldn't say it openly to an audience of psychoanalysts. I would likely have been subjected to analysis right then and there." He acknowledged the weakness of his joke with a faint smile.

"Do you mean you've met him?"

"Of course," the priest replied with great seriousness.

"Are you an exorcist by any chance?"

"Nothing of the kind. I'm talking about the devil-made-man, flesh and blood like me and you."

"How can that be? I mean, a devil registered in the census, complete with name and surname, driver's license and health-care card."

The priest frowned.

"The one does not exclude the other. In fact for all intents and purposes he is a man: he is born of a father and a mother, almost always pious, decent people who accept the burden of such an offspring as expiation. Others, however, can't tolerate it and manage to get rid of the devil when he is still in swaddling clothes. That's why many of them are foundlings, children abandoned by their parents, not out of economic necessity, but for having manifested their malevolent nature from the very first days of their lives. And ultimately they are adopted by childless couples longing to have a baby. The devil thus exploits his parasitic position, and most of the time he causes his parents' deaths, whether by a simulated accident or a broken heart, so he can inherit their possessions and dedicate himself to his own mission. A devil's career, however, is not always crowned with success. Very often these subjects, whom we might rightly call poor devils, have a short life, and most times they end up behind bars where there are few opportunities to exercise their evil arts. On the other hand, many are born into legitimate, aristocratic families, who suspect nothing of their scions' peculiar natures, often justifying and even encouraging their unseemly behavior, as if it were a mark of power. And these individuals procreate actual diabolical genealogies. We don't know how many of them there are roaming around the world. Probably many more than we think."

"And how can they be recognized?"

"There are signs that presage an evil nature. Recurrent signs that not everyone is able to recognize, however."

"For example?"

"They are behaviors that are manifested from early childhood, such as a tendency toward excessive lying, or gratuitous cruelty toward animals. Of course, all children lie to avoid punishment, or because they live in an imaginary world, just as everyone has a legitimate curiosity to find out how a living creature is made inside, but when dissection becomes a habitual practice and its purpose is solely to inflict pain, in that case the child requires vigilance. Anyway, that's the most obvious sign, but there are dozens of others that develop later on, which there's no need to speak of. One says it all: the ability to make your thoughts turn against you."

Father Cornelius seemed to search my face to study the effect of his statement. Reading a trace of skepticism there, he continued:

"First the Church, and later romantic literature, gave the devil prominence: they portrayed him in various ways, they gave him a face, a character, they provided him with a job, a mission, they clothed him in all kinds of attire, to the degree of making him visible, alive. In short, they humanized him."

I wasn't sure where he was going with this. I felt like I was listening to the ravings of a madman. In any case, I played along.

"So the devil was created in our image and likeness?"

"Precisely. There is nothing in the world that was not first conceived of by a mind, even before it existed. You write, I suppose ..."

Taken by surprise, as if writing were a sin to be ashamed of, I felt myself redden: "Is it obvious by looking at me?"

"It's not hard to see," Father Cornelius replied with a smile, "and besides, last night I heard the clacking of a typewriter."

It was true: the night before, right after supper, I had gone up to my room to make a clean copy of some notes scrawled in pencil in a notebook. I had typed a few lines on my old portable, but then, thinking it was too noisy for that quiet place, I had put it back in its case. But the fact that my secret passion was written on my face didn't sit too well with me.

"I'm trying at least, with no appreciable results," I replied, with some embarrassment.

"You are still young and have every possibility ahead of

you. But be careful about the choices you make."

"What do you mean?"

"Literature is the greatest of the arts," the priest continued, "but it is also a dangerous endeavor."

"In what sense, dangerous?"

"Each time we pick up a pen we are preparing to perform a ritual for which two candles should always be lit: one white and one black. Unlike painting and sculpture, which remain anchored to a material subject, and to music, which in contrast transcends matter altogether, literature can dominate both spheres: the concrete and the abstract, the terrestrial and the otherworldly. Moreover, it propagates and multiplies with infinite variations in readers' minds. Without knowing it, the writer can become a formidable egregore."

"Egregore? What's that?"

The priest assumed a patient attitude.

"Today the meaning of the term has been greatly diminished. It means a chain reaction caused by univocal thinking. There is an exemplary tale about it: it is said that in an old friars' monastery a gust of wind had lifted into the air a monk's habit that had been laid out to dry in the sun. After a brief flight the garment glided like a kite to the bottom of a crag, getting tangled in the branches of a bush not far from the path that the friars took early in the morning on their daily walk. And each day, in the monks' imaginations, that habit increasingly assumed the form of a man. Someone then suggested that it could be the devil, stationed at that spot to count souls. From that moment on, in the mind of the monks, the figure grew more and more menacing, until it took on material form and drove the whole monastery into a frenzy. And only the bishop's intervention was able to make the devil go away and resume his earlier form: that of a mere bush. The writer, therefore, can initiate a chain of thought capable of attributing life and intelligence even to a figure everyone considers to be imaginary, such as the devil."

At that precise moment we heard the front door of the inn open. Someone had come in, but from the spot where we were sitting we could not see him. Only his heavy steps could be heard treading the floorboards; evidently he was a customer who had stopped for a drink. For a moment the man appeared in the doorway of the dining room, his profile filling the entire space. Seeing him, I jumped in my seat. The man, in fact, was the same fellow I had run into in the woods, busily flinging that gory pulp on the ground. This time, however, his menacing figure was refined by a clean shirt, revealing a brawny neck, and a checked jacket that seemed to have been made out of a full-size bedspread. Since no one showed up, we heard him stomp out, muttering between his teeth. Father Cornelius looked me straight in the eye.

"Speaking of the devil ..."

I burst into a nervous little laugh: "I ran across that man this morning."

"His name is Hans," the priest explained, "and he is the local veterinarian's assistant. At this time he is assigned to perform a truly distasteful task."

"The task of scattering ... what? Poisoned bait?"

Father Cornelius shook his head: "Despite his appearance, Hans is a gentle, sensitive man, who loves animals very much—which makes his task doubly unpleasant: not only must he prepare that disgusting pulp with his own hands, but he must also obtain the raw ingredients."

"Which would be?"

"Fox cubs."

"You mean baby foxes?"

"He catches them in their dens and doesn't hesitate to cut them into bits and pieces. To that end he always carries a cleaver and a wooden chopping board hanging from his belt. Only the smell of their murdered offspring keeps the rabid foxes away from the villages."

Hearing those words I felt my stomach turn, but Father Cornelius didn't seem to notice it and went on as if nothing had happened.

"A fox infected with rabies," he said, "behaves strangely: he doesn't run away at the sight of a man, but approaches him effusively until he is able to bite him. And so, too, the devil: his first strategy, in fact, is to become friendly with the designated victim. Therefore, the first rule of defense is to not let yourself be deceived by appearances. Nowadays the devil no longer has horns, nor a two-sided cape, he no longer smells of sulfur, he doesn't frighten us with his façade, but rather he does everything he can to make himself seem helpful and agreeable. He doesn't have, as one might think, the look of a huckster, nor of an eye-winking panderer, nor that of a jolly good fellow with an inexhaustible repertoire of spicy stories. His appearance is always well-groomed, he wears double-breasted suits, his speech is refined, his tone of voice persuasive. Except for one detail that escapes attention at the moment. Nonetheless it is perceived subliminally and makes him appear ridiculous. It's like seeing a price tag still attached to the jacket of someone who prides himself on displaying a sophisticated elegance. But too bad for anyone who notices this detail, or rather, too bad if he is discovered to have noticed it, because this will send the devil into a rage, and then that individual will become his target. The devil is extremely touchy, in fact. Being the low man on the totem pole, on the bottom rung of the infernal hierarchy, he is thus even more motivated to get ahead; in other words, he is the prototype of the corporal who aspires to one day become the great general. But like all of us, even the devil has to come to terms with History and its changes. Owing to the progress of science and technology, the ground shifted beneath his feet, and before long he had to accept modernity, or rather, resign himself to not being up to the sudden changes in our century. These days the great stages of the past, with their fascinating sets exalting his figure, no longer exist; the imposing cathedrals are replaced by churches designed by less than mediocre architects, the grand theaters are as unadorned as parish chapels, and the somber castles, when not completely ruined, are invaded by noisy crowds of little brats, accompanied by parents who roam the halls with their Baedekers in hand and noses in the air. Given such a scenario, what's left to the poor old-school devil? What does he have to do to avoid being outclassed by the new diabolical generations? By this time he is too old to be able to be refashioned—that's right, because even the devil incarnate is accordingly subjected to earthly laws: he ages, he goes out of style, he loses his shine, he gets sick and finally dies, damned as he was at birth. The scope of his operations has been greatly curtailed, his magic tricks are now outmoded: the world of so-called spiritual power is out of his reach, as is that of financial power, which is now the prerogative of corrupt politics; what's left to him, therefore, is merely power as an end in itself, that which is exercised in any human congregation where there is competition. It could be the neighborhood bowling league or the most exclusive Rotary club. But all the better if it is a pseudo-intellectual competition. Consequently, the ideal place is a literary society, not only because literature is the last locus of knowledge that still attributes him a certain credibility, but also because it is the place where vainglory, fueled by envy, grows immoderately, where even the most banal thoughts—as long as they are printed in type—are accepted as absolute truth."

I was beginning to feel uncomfortable, because an activity dear to me, to which I thought I would devote myself entirely in the future, was under accusation.

"In your opinion, then, literature is bad?"

After his unexpected outburst, Father Cornelius composed himself and, having regained his calm, proceeded in a more even tone.

"It is not my intention to divert you from your fervent passion, nor to question the significance and value of literature. As I have already said, it is the most sublime of the arts. And your question as to whether literature is bad leaves me perplexed; it would be like asking whether man himself isn't bad; since literature is man's most genuine and profound expression, it contains all human wretchedness, as well as its greatness. However, it is not art that I want to speak about so much as the weaknesses of its practitioners and the passions that devour them, making them easy prey for the Evil One. There are countless types of writers, whom I picture as so many cooks: I see them bent over their stoves, intent on creating their special delicacies, consummate gourmet chefs and barracks cooks alike. Just put a pen in their hand in place of a ladle and the taxonomy of literati will appear plainly before us, classifiable in family, genus, species, and so on, all intent on simmering their ideas over a slow fire, possessive of their secret recipes, willing to bend over backwards for a horde of gluttons, notwithstanding their noble and professional titles: people with a cardboard palate, ready to move their jaws just to grind up food and inflate their stomachs, people who at the end of the meal feel bound to crush out a cigarette in the immaculate cream of a slice of Saint Honoré. There, don't you agree that this image reflects what literary society is?"

Actually, I'd had enough of his disquisitions on the literati.

"I wouldn't know, since I don't belong to any literary society, nor have I ever belonged to one."

"Good for you. Stay away from those dens of iniquity. It is often in those kitchens that the devil can be found. And I assure you that you cannot expect him to show a shred of gratitude toward them. Indeed, it is precisely the literati that he is most angry with. It is as if he wanted to destroy the source from which he originated, to erase all evidence of having been created by a handful of brilliant albeit injudicious writers. I can tell you this from experience: I know a place, in fact, where a whole colony of writers was overcome by a particularly enterprising devil."

At those words, I pricked up my ears. Was he about to tell me a story? I didn't dare hope for it.

"Oh really? And where did this happen?" I asked, with the intention of getting him to talk.

Just then we were interrupted by the waitress who, after having cleared the tables, came to give us some instructions. It was clear that she couldn't wait to leave; she was probably already late for an appointment. She informed us that she would lock the front door, but since we were the only ones staying at the hotel, we were certainly welcome to stay where we were. Should we need it, we had the key to the service door. Father Cornelius took the opportunity to order a mug of beer ... or rather two, one for me as well. Everything led me to think that he wanted to keep me there a little longer.

To this day, when I think back to the moment when Father Cornelius proposed to tell me his story, I wonder what my life would have been like if I had decided not to listen to him, if I had declined his offer and made some excuse to retire to my room. In that case, perhaps, I might have become a writer as I had always dreamed of being. I would have followed my path, I would have cultivated the length and breadth of my farm, however modest its area might have been, without encroaching on other people's property, surely more vast and unexplored, but also littered with ravines and perilous shifting sands. But for an aspiring writer, a story told by a stranger is like manna from heaven. The temptation was too strong. Nothing and nobody would have persuaded me to decline. And since I seemed quite willing to listen to him, the priest began his account.

1

I won't tell you the name of the place where this tragi-comic affair took place. In fact, it is my intention to misdirect you as far as possible. This is to protect the good name of those who were my parishioners. The events that occurred, in fact, are not at all edifying; it is difficult to believe that, because of the devil, an entire community, in the grip of collective hysteria, became drawn into a series of incidents that transport us back to the Middle Ages. Someday perhaps you may discover this location on your own, but the moral of the story would not change in any case. Therefore, consider what I am about to tell you a simple parable.

The village I'm talking about is situated in a canton in Switzerland. I'll give it a predictable name: I'd say *Dichters-ruhe* ("poet's repose") suits it perfectly. Dichtersruhe is nestled in a deep, narrow valley, nearly suffocated by the mountains, cut in two by a stream that often swells with the rains and that roars all year round, except in rare dry periods. The landscape's aspect reflects the character of its inhabitants: welcoming in the summer, severe and cruel in the cold season. Dichtersruhe is a district of a larger center, yet even today it remains far more important than the center of which it is a part, for the simple reason that Goethe stayed there for one night, I believe, or perhaps two—the time it took the local blacksmith to repair the wheel hub of the carriage in which the poet was traveling. The allure of tourism was far too tempting, so that more than a century later people began exploiting the poet's name, attributing to themselves the distinction of having hosted him. Even today there are no less than three inns in contention for the honor, though you'd need only consult the land register to find that there weren't any real inns in Dichtersruhe at that time, and that perhaps Goethe found hospitality with a family sufficiently well-off to have a room available for the rare travelers who passed through the valley. Only at the start of the twentieth century did the hotel business as we know it today begin. It is not really clear, therefore, how this belief originated. Nevertheless, it has been handed down from generation to generation, gaining strength over the course of the centuries. No less than three inns, the Gasthof Meyer, the Gasthof Webern, and the Pension Müller, still contend this privilege today: three inns with as many rooms and as many beds in which the landlords are prepared to swear that the illustrious guest, on his way from Weimar and perhaps headed for Italy, supposedly rested from his tiring journey. Only one of the three, however, can boast of a detail—perhaps the innkeeper's brilliant idea—that makes its claim more credible: a sturdy nail with a rectangular head, affixed to the wall next to the entrance door, a rough coat hook on which the celebrated writer is said to have hung his overcoat when he crossed the threshold. Under this relic, venerated as if it were a nail of the Cross, is a brass plaque engraved with the presumed date of the event and, next to it, a sheet of parchment bearing an aphorism attributed to Goethe: *art is long, life is short, judgment difficult.*

I returned to Dichtersruhe recently, after an absence of ten years. Seemingly nothing had changed, and yet I was able to roam through the streets and enter a tavern without meeting anyone I used to know. Stone endures, lives pass on: some died, others moved away, the former children are now adults and perhaps don't even remember the episode of collective madness that struck the entire community. In other respects, Dichtersruhe has remained as it was. In summer it is a charming, picture-postcard place. Even today, from June to August, when the inns are filled with vacationers, the whole village is revived, and various street markets are set up in the central square, offering handcrafted specialties; among them, in place of the usual dolls in traditional costume, the figure of Goethe, carved in stone pine or sculpted in clay, is by far the most prevalent. Crafts are an activity that elderly people and children have always engaged in during the winter months. The most talented are able to reproduce the famous painting by Tischbein, the one that portrays the poet reclining on a chaise-longue in the middle of the Roman countryside. And so what if his calf sometimes appears a bit stubby, or if the hand is vaguely sketched, so that it looks like he's wearing a woolen mitten? Everyone contrives to do the best he can; besides, there is no lack of subjects to tackle. Found for sale, therefore, are various versions of the poet's bust, bas-relief portraits that more or less resemble him, and even countless variations of his mortuary mask, along with hand-painted plates that depict some of his aphorisms. For the rest, the town has no particular attractions, and no ski resorts either—you have to travel quite a few kilometers to find facilities equipped for winter tourism. Dichtersruhe thus remains a place for indolent hikers who, posing as expert rock climbers, love to clamber up wooded slopes that present no risk. Nearby there is also a health resort with a thermal spring, a real cure-all for the kidneys. The Kursaal is distinguished by a cluster of charming pine wood lodges, painted green, whose pagoda roofs are topped with tin weather vanes, some of which creak at each alpine zephyr. The restitution—so to speak—of ingested liquids takes place, weather permitting, outside the lodges, where there are rows of deckchairs arranged not too far from the urinals.

In addition to the three inns, almost every family offers a room to rent with half-board. Located in the center of the square, in front of the café Oetker—which is also an excellent restaurant—is a bronze statue of Goethe, the work of a famous Swiss sculptor. Placed on a marble pedestal, the statue, two meters in height, represents the poet standing, wearing a frock coat, a wide-brimmed hat, and cuffed, calf-high boots. One hand leans on a walking stick and the other holds a sheaf of papers. His noble profile is turned upwards, looking toward the mountains, as if he wanted to orient himself as to which path to take. Perennially exposed to the elements, the statue is occasionally cloaked in white on snowy days, or adorned with icicles, while on certain rainy winter days that turn to radiant blue the gleaming bronze seems to capture the last ray of the setting sun. From time to time a raven perches on the poet's shoulder, as if to suggest a verse to

him, or a great tit nests for a season under the wing of his
hat.

2

It was Dichtersruhe to which I was assigned as vicar ten years ago by the diocese, to assist the man who had been the parish priest for over half a century, and who, despite being well over ninety, had not yet made up his mind to retire. I was therefore supposed to act in his place, performing tasks that had become too taxing for him. In reality I was in all respects his substitute, since he confined himself to a rare appearance on only the most important occasions, and the rest of the time remained closeted in his apartment to write—as I would later discover—his memoirs.

I had been assigned the part of the rectory that faced north, with a stark bedroom and a small, modest study that had remained empty all those years. The rectory's housekeeper, who for fifty years had faithfully tended to the priest, saw to our meals. We did not, however, share the same table: I ate in the kitchen under the old woman's grim eye, and the pastor had his meals brought to him in his study, which he rarely left. Despite his age, except for a certain weakness in the legs, he still enjoyed good health.

He had a plump face, accentuated by thick white eyebrows, and a red, spongy nose that made one doubt his sobriety. His name was Father Cristoforo.

He rarely received me in his study, and then only to give me brisk orders. His room was a comfortable retreat: fir-paneled walls, a coffered ceiling, shelves full of books, even a fireplace that looked promising. His desk was entirely covered with papers, which he seemed very possessive of. One day when I'd leaned over a bit too far to take a peek at one of those papers, he'd whisked it out of sight so quickly that I felt hurt. I was sure he did not look well upon me, that he even considered me an intruder. For my part, I felt more and more depressed in that place. Used to city life, finding myself in a village of a thousand souls was unbearable. Moreover, I knew very well that the reason for my transfer had been the rumors about me. Rumors completely false, but that, properly fueled by a chorus of malicious voices, had over time assumed a strong undertone of truth, convincing the bishop to sequester me in this valley.

I realized right away that I would not have an easy time with my parishioners: I could tell from the low turnout at services and at confession. After fifty years with the same parish priest they were convinced that they had earned a plenary indulgence for life. For half a century they had bared their souls to Father Cristoforo, and it seemed pointless to them to start all over again with a newcomer whom they could not be entirely sure would keep their secrets. When it was I who celebrated Sunday Mass, the church was half empty; it only filled up with the presence of the old pastor. Every enthusiastic attempt I made to socialize with the local people was dampened by indifference, every proposal I made to bring young people together by instituting painting, acting, music, or other classes was blatantly shunned. As a substitute for Father Cristoforo, who by now almost never left the rectory, I occupied his seat in the town council, but I remained in effect an insignificant bystander; being new to the place, I was unable to express an opinion, which, furthermore, no one cared to know.

The inhabitants of Dichtersruhe were almost all related to one another. The oldest and most prevalent names were Meyer, Müller, and Webern. Other surnames followed, less frequent in the district but rather common in Switzerland, such as Schwartz, Keller, Linz, and so on. Of course there were many Meyers who had married a Webern or a Müller, and vice versa, forming a dense network of descendants, where the males all bore the grandfather's baptismal name, and very often that of the father, so that to distinguish someone with certainty it was necessary to resort to nicknames; all of them were given one, and though it sometimes corresponded to their trade, more often it was a humorous moniker whose origin was incomprehensible even to the person who bore it. Since certain names, transmitted from generation to generation, had completely lost their literal significance over time, those who, like me, heard them for the first time could not help but smile at the thought that there were Bellyscratcher Weberns, Shit-scared Müllers, or worse yet.

During the summer months the villagers still extended a certain cordiality toward me, but as the days grew shorter this waned in correlation with the sun's lowering path, until it disappeared altogether in the winter season. At that time each individual turned inward, isolating himself from the others. This made my job difficult, since my work required me to maintain close relations with people, a task that sometimes seemed hopeless to me. Naturally, I went knocking door to door, I visited every house to deliver my blessing, but I constantly ran up against the strictest reserve. Not one person thought of inviting me to sit down, of offering me a glass of water, or at least giving me a smile ... Actually I did get one smile, albeit sarcastic, from a man who, when I went to his house, asked me if blessings, like food products, had an expiration date, and if by chance the blessing given by Father Cristoforo some time back was no longer considered valid.

Harsh people, the sheep in my flock, withdrawn, surly individuals, bound—one would have said—by a secret pact dating back to a distant past. It was clear that no one was well-disposed toward outsiders. Even tourists, who represented a significant part of the local economy, were barely tolerated, considered a necessary evil, and everyone breathed a sigh of relief upon seeing them leave at the end of summer. As long as they filled the rooms of an inn and bought the local products, they could still be stomached, but too bad if any of those rich moneybags from the big cities got it into his head to ask if there was any land for sale for building a vacation home, or a dilapidated ruin to be restored. Then he would come up against an insurmountable wall of silence. So it was quite understandable that in the eyes of the inhabitants I was an intruder, sent there purposely to replace the beloved figure of the parish priest, or in any case to bring about changes that no one would welcome. It is well known that a people's character is conditioned by the setting, yet this explanation did not wholly satisfy me. There was something else that continued to elude me: the inhabitants of Dichtersruhe all seemed to be under the influence of a spell. And it was by pure chance that I was able to unveil the mystery.

3

One day I was at the post office to mail some letters for the parish priest, when through the glass window at the counter I noticed a parcel on its way out, addressed to a publishing house. I also clearly saw the name of the sender, a certain Hans Schwartz who lived at the edge of the village and who was a swine gelder by trade. What that individual had to do with Schuster & Schuster in Berlin I could not imagine. The only plausible explanation was that it was to express second thoughts about a subscription to purchase a costly book series. The episode would have been forgotten if only a week later, once more at the post office, something hadn't again aroused my curiosity. I was standing in line at the counter and in front of me was Joseph Müller, the baker. He hadn't noticed me, so I was able to peer over his shoulder. He was holding a large envelope, reinforced on the edges with adhesive tape. He held it close to his chest, but I still managed to read the name of the recipient: this time it was Kriegel Verlag in Munich.

Realizing that I was behind him, he suddenly seemed to

reconsider and did an about-face just as he was handing over the envelope. Snatching it out of the clerk's hand, visibly embarrassed, he left the post office. I understood immediately that the reason for his strange behavior was my presence. In the time it had taken for the clerk to apply the stamps and postmark, I'd been able to read the address and the name to which the package was being sent. Not to take any chances, Müller had preferred to take it back home. All this seemed extremely bizarre to me, to the extent that I decided to investigate more thoroughly. Around noon, when the square was more crowded, I stationed myself near the post office, where there appeared to be intense activity. And lo and behold, one day one of the Meyers went in holding a large envelope to be mailed, colliding in the doorway with one of the Weberns, who had just picked up an envelope similar to that of Meyer. There was, therefore, a steady coming and going of outgoing and incoming mail. Really unusual for a village of a thousand souls! To make a long story short, thanks also to the complicity of the new postmaster, an irreverent young man from the city who couldn't care less about privacy, I discovered that everyone in Dichtersruhe wrote, or at least that there wasn't a single family that did not count an aspiring writer in its midst. Incredible! Everyone was a poet, short-story writer, historian, or novelist ... There was no other place in the world with such a high number of would-be writers. And they all submitted their manuscripts to the large publishing houses, which invariably rejected them and returned them to the sender. No one got discouraged, however—the patience of the valley's inhabitants is proverbial. They went on writing their novels, poems, memoirs, and so on, and simply started over again with another publisher. Everyone wrote about everything in Dichtersruhe, and it wasn't just the living who claimed their rights, but also the dead. And so every scrap of paper on which something was printed or written—from correspondence among relatives to contracts for the sale of land or livestock—was exhumed and preserved to be able to draw something new from it about the history of the family or of the village itself. Although two centuries had gone by since the great poet had passed through there, in spirit he was still present as a tutelary deity; everyone felt illuminated by the light of that comet, and invested with a common mission. The art of writing did not differ much from that of sculpting wood or clay, and each individual, according to his own proclivity, sought to do the best he could, modestly, without any fanciful literary notions, without any ambitious goals. In appearance at least, writing was a pastime, a recreational activity available to anyone who wanted to give it a try, with no animosity toward those who cultivated the same passion. Until then no one had distinguished himself, and the flock lived peacefully, each member grazing his own small plot of land. It is true that in their hearts they would not have turned their noses up at even a slim shred of recognition, but that was a deeply buried hope, held in check, and, if anything, only fantasized about in their most intimate dreams. In terms of probability, therefore, contacting the big publishers amounted to attempting one's luck in the national lottery. In any case, it was indeed a fine satisfaction to receive a letter that usually ended with the words: *although we appreciated your work, at this time we must decline it. We wish you better luck, etc., etc.*

Many of these letters were framed and hung on the wall, as certificates of merit.

4

Having discovered this innocent secret, I was more inclined to judge my parishioners with greater benevolence. It was a new awareness that made me look at people differently, trying to guess which category they belonged to. Could burgomaster Keller, for example, be a novelist? Or was he a historian? Or maybe a fan of the detective genre? Though I had managed to become somewhat friendly with him, nothing was revealed from our conversations, which usually revolved around international politics. And could the wife of cantonal councilman Linz, so sophisticated in her style of dress, with her elegant French "r," be writing a romantic love story in her free time? And who could have imagined that the grocer Bauer was the author of a science-fiction trilogy? My brain now operated on a one-way track: at the café Oetker, where I went to look at the newspapers, I would strain my ears to try to hear what was being said at the nearby tables. Though they were perhaps talking about sports or politics, I had the impression that the subject of the conversations, filtered through my mind's obsessed fixation, was always the same single one: great literature.

I began to feel a touch of sympathy, even toward the parish priest. Nevertheless I couldn't help wondering what was so interesting about those thousands of pages written over the years by a man who had never stepped foot out of Dichtersruhe.

The discovery of my parishioners' secret passion gave me the opportunity to establish a closer relationship with them. I began to draw their attention by increasingly touching upon the theme of art, and especially literature, in my sermons. And it was not long before I saw that I had pressed the right button. In a short time, I found the church full of faithful followers.

By then my Sunday sermons referred to nothing else, and they were therefore very well attended. I spoke about the difficult course that writers and poets had had to endure in the past, and who only after their deaths had been accorded the well-deserved consecration of the public and of critics. I recounted the lives of genuine talents who had not been recognized in their lifetimes because of the myopia of their contemporaries. I tried to highlight the positive aspect that a rejection or a defeat can represent in the development of an artistic personality. Most of my sermons were nothing more than literature lessons, but I did not fail to urge them to raise their guard against all the temptations that the devil might arouse in them, through pride and envy, and other dangers that may lurk in an activity which, in its pursuit of beauty, should be a reward sufficient in itself. Goethe came to my rescue, and I often read entire passages from *Faust*. What an endless wealth of reflections this poem contained! And as I spoke from the pulpit, I could see the faces of my parishioners light up like candle wicks touched by the passage of a flame. From their expressions it was easy to tell what their secret passion was. Even the three oldest families of the village began to attend Sunday Mass: the Müllers, the Meyers, and the Weberns, who owned the three inns that vied for the privilege of having hosted Goethe. There was no trace of rancor among them. All three families were in good faith, all three convinced that they were right. And only Goethe would have been able to say how things transpired. Despite contending for that honor, they did not do so to profit from it: they had no lack of customers, in fact, a sign indicating "no vacancy" hung above the entrances all summer long. So there had never been any friction among them, on the contrary, on many occasions they had unanimously fostered initiatives to keep the memory of that distant event alive, and they had even agreed to contribute to the bronze casting of the poet's statue out of their own pockets. Nevertheless, a covert competition was always afoot, and if the name of one of the three families were to appear on the frontispiece of a book published in thousands of copies by a prominent publishing house, that would have dispelled all doubt with regard to the age-old question.

5

It is not entirely clear how Dichtersruhe, that godforsaken village tucked into one of the many Swiss valleys, could have attracted the devil's attention. I imagine it was because of that spark of notoriety that struck the entire village following the award received by a local inhabitant who won a national competition for children's literature. The winner was not one of the Meyers, nor the Weberns, much less the Müllers, but to everyone's great surprise it was Marta, the only daughter of the widow Bauer, a young girl whom all the villagers considered to be mentally retarded. It was said that the cause of her deficiency was a bizarre accident that her mother had had when she was eight months pregnant: one night, the worm-eaten legs of the massive chest of drawers in the bedroom had suddenly given way and the bureau had toppled forward, smashing to pieces on the floor. The poor woman was so frightened that her waters broke, and after a difficult birth, due to the unhappy position of the fetus, she'd given birth to a puny, cyanotic creature whose umbilical cord was wrapped twice around her neck; only after several minutes had the infant begun to show the first signs of life. Deprived for too long of an essential supply of oxygen, the baby girl's brain suffered grave harm, precluding any possibility of her having a normal life in the future.

At the time of these events Marta was twenty-five years old and had lived as a recluse inside the walls of an Ursuline convent where she'd been assigned the most humble tasks—that is, until a wall collapsed due to water penetration, compromising the stability of the entire building and forcing the nuns to find a different home. By the time she left the convent she was already a woman, but she was so small and frail in appearance that she looked like a girl of thirteen. At a time when many women of her age had long been married and had given birth to children, Marta seemed marked by all those years spent in the convent. She regarded men with implacable amazement: she saw them as grotesque representations of the female gender carried to its extreme; she couldn't bear their raised voices and flat breasts, the hair on their faces, not to mention the protuberance whose functions some joker had told her about, provoking her unrestrained laughter. Marta almost never left the house, except in the company of her mother, and the places where she spent most of her time were the kitchen and the vegetable garden behind the house. The nuns had taught her to read and write, but her great passion was painting, and in particular, watercolor. During those years of isolation she had developed her own personal poetic world, bringing to life everyday objects such as spoons, knives, and forks, and combining them with plants, fruit trees, and insects from the garden where, during the summer, she spent most of her time.

Until then no one had ever suspected that this retarded

girl could secretly cultivate a talent capable of one day giving her a moment of glory. The three oldest families in the village could not resign themselves to this blatant injustice, and raised their eyes to heaven with an expression of reproach. Could Goethe have wished to put an end to their interminable dispute in a way worthy of Solomon, inspiring a poor demented woman instead of them? The fact is that the case of Marta Bauer quickly filled the pages of the newspapers: her simple nursery rhymes recounting tales of love between vegetables and flowers, illustrated with great skill, had earned her first prize. In any case, all of Dichtersruhe benefited: for a few weeks, numerous reporters from various newspapers arrived on the scene, even from abroad. A great many photographs were taken of the three inns in contention, and very soon the story of Marta Bauer and the village of literati, marked by Goethe's dazzling passage, was in the public eye.

This news could not have escaped a poor devil who, having been unemployed for some time, wanted nothing more than to undertake a new venture. Dichtersruhe had become a pond teeming with disillusioned fish, worn out by waiting, where it would be worthwhile to cast his net.

And the fact that his arrival coincided with a sudden outbreak of wild rabies did not seem like a coincidence to me at all.

Today as well as then, I have always believed in premonitions, and I'm not talking about those associated with popular superstition, such as: if you break a mirror you can expect seven years of hard luck, or if you walk under a ladder something bad will happen to you, and so on. Rather I believe in those signs that come from nature, as unequivocal as the plagues of Egypt: a sudden epidemic among livestock, the inexplicable widespread death of birds, an invasion of insects ...

True, wild rabies exists and has always existed. However, it remains within certain limits. But when an endemic disease has a sudden fresh outbreak, when rabid foxes seem to lay siege to your village, roaming the streets at night, entering courtyards and scratching at doors, when not even rifle fire scares them off, then yes, you can certainly think of it as a grim premonition, or perhaps even a divine warning.

6

That was what happened in Dichtersruhe the spring following my transfer there. The first signs were seen in a dog that exhibited suspicious symptoms. The animal had always been kept chained in a courtyard, and therefore could only have been attacked on site. The occurrence went almost unnoticed, in part because there was not an accurate diagnosis by a veterinarian. Yet two weeks later several foxes were spotted in the village, and other domestic animals were infected. By now it was May and the arrival of the first tourists was just over a month away. There was therefore the danger that the epidemic might reach its peak at the very height of summer, and no one wanted to take it upon himself to alarm the passionate hikers who came to Dichtersruhe in droves, particularly to enjoy long walks in the woods. Barring the paths and denying people access to the infested areas was unthinkable, but neither could they be left in the dark about the risks they'd be taking. Indeed, because there was no longer any doubt: this time the local veterinarian had laboratory tests performed that confirmed the presence of the virus.

The burgomaster didn't wait to be asked twice and immediately alerted hunters to go track down the foxes and exterminate their offspring. Despite careful searches, only a few burrows were found, empty, since the pups had already been moved elsewhere or, perhaps, as a last resort, devoured by their own mothers. All in all, not a single fox was sighted. And yet, as soon as evening came on, their shadows could be glimpsed prowling close to the walls. People barricaded themselves in their homes, and in the middle of the night the foxes' shrill baying could be heard coming from the forest. What sounds came from those jaws! A horrific symphony, so unbearable that I had to plug my ears so as not to go crazy. By then I felt my nerves would not be able to take it much longer. I managed to sleep only a few hours a night, and during the day I jumped like a spring at the slightest noise ...

Lest my reaction seem excessive, I feel the need to explain the reason for it. There are certain deeply rooted fears in us that we can never free ourselves of. There are those who shudder at just the thought of a spider, who faint at the sight of a mouse, or a snake ... Well, I confess, to this day I have a physiological horror of foxes, a horror that I have never been able to overcome, despite being convinced of having identified its cause. I am positive that this phobia springs from an episode that occurred in my early childhood. At the time I had been given a dog, a young setter with whom I often spent entire days. His only fault was to give in to his hunting instinct, disappearing from home and returning several days later. The last time, however, his absence went on for too long. After a week of hoping, my father took me aside to tell me that it was pointless to keep waiting for the dog and that I had to make my peace with it, because the setter would certainly not come back. I cried and despaired at the thought that I would never see him again. And maybe it would have been better that way, because after a few weeks away the dog returned. Or rather, what remained of him returned. One day, as I was looking dejectedly out the window, I saw him, sitting in the tall grass. He seemed to be waiting for me ... I rushed outside and ran toward him. I immediately thought it was strange, however, that he did not react in any way to my call: he remained stock-still in the grass. He didn't move, not even when I was but a few meters from him. Right away I saw that he was in a pitiful state: sores all over his body, reduced to skin and bone. But when I held out my hand to have him recognize me, the dog rushed at me, trying to bite, and it was only due to his extreme weakness that he did not succeed in his intent. Leaping back I was able to dodge his attack, but his reaction had scared me to death and I burst into tears. At that moment something happened that I would never forget: the poor animal, torn between two opposing natures at war in him, prostrated himself at my feet and began to whimper piteously, as if begging my forgiveness for his having tried to hurt me, as if wanting to alert me because the evil nature in him was about to gain the upper hand. I don't remember anything else except that my father ran over in time to carry me to safety. It was he who told me that it had been the bite of a fox that had reduced the dog to that state. And since that time, that elegant little creature the fox has been transformed in my mind into a terrible disease-spreader, a carrier of rabies, the very emblem of evil. He has populated my worst nightmares, and has become my most deep-seated phobia, to the degree of even causing my faith to waver. That's right, because that episode contained within it the mystery of human nature.

Was evil transmittable? Was it contagious? What was the use of pursuing good when it could be convulsed by a simple scratch or a trickle of foam at the mouth?

During the time when the foxes' siege continued relentlessly, my doubts became stronger and stronger. And perhaps I would not have held up under the tension and would have fled the village, had the phenomenon not ceased as abruptly as it had begun. The foxes retreated to the forest, restoring peace to the inhabitants of Dichtersruhe. Some explained the fact by citing the changing phase of the moon, others credited the parish priest's paternosters, or the procession of Saint Martha, the village's patron saint; or perhaps one could simply consider that the disease had run its natural course, and that after reaching its maximum peak it had regressed on its own. Every possible precaution was taken, however: animals suspected of having been infected were put down and thrown into a large pit dug in a remote spot, where they were covered with quicklime before being buried. The villagers were still incredulous; it seemed like a virtual miracle that the tourist season, now almost upon them, was no longer in danger of being compromised.

If the phenomenon had ceased, it was because the devil had already set foot in the area. But only I knew about his arrival. Now it was a matter of identifying him, a job that could prove to be no small task. Then too, one had to wonder how he would act, what strategy he would apply to a peaceful community of valley-dwellers characterized by such a cautious, suspicious nature.

7

When you think about it, what is the key that is capable of forcing the mind of an aspiring writer who has tried everything without result? You have to appeal to his vanity, recognize the misunderstood genius in him, present yourself as a thaumaturgist capable of proposing remedies, of restoring hope, of recreating illusions ... and for an aspiring writer, who more than an obliging publisher possesses all of these qualities? It was just the thing in a village of literati: all they needed was a devil of a publisher who, coming from God knows where, would invade Dichtersruhe like a fox in a henhouse. So there was really no need to look for him, because it was he who manifested himself to the community in the most blatant way imaginable. Of course he knew quite well whom to start with: after having systematically persuaded burgomaster Keller, an exponent of temporal power, he moved on to the next phase, launching the first attack on spiritual authority. He requested a meeting with the village's parish priest, a meeting which, in my capacity as vicar, I could not possibly miss. Father Cristoforo had already been informed of his arrival, and that morning he appeared unusually excited. He came into the kitchen several times to give instructions to the housekeeper, and meeting me on the stairs, he announced delightedly that we were to be visited by an important figure, who might stay for lunch. At the time I thought of some illustrious cleric who, passing through, had deigned to visit our small mountain parish. I could not yet imagine that I would soon run into the devil himself. I immediately realized it was him when I saw him arrive escorted by a municipal delegation. I would not have been surprised to see a brass-band as well. Only he and the burgomaster came inside. After greeting Father Cristoforo, bowing in an attempt to kiss his ring—a gesture to which the pastor, pleasantly confused, offered only weak resistance—, the devil turned to me.

"Bernhard Fuchs," he said, holding out his hand, which I was careful not to touch. I responded with a slight bow, while pressing my right hand to my chest as if to hide a split seam or a missing button.

"Publisher from Lucerne," he added, his arm ossified in mid-air, but I remained unmoving until I saw him withdraw his hand, skillfully disguising the humiliation. Still, all he had to do was say his name, "Bernard Fox," and it made my blood run cold.

Hard to believe it's a coincidence, I thought. Maybe I was wrong not to shake his hand, but that very common gesture also serves to sanction a pact—the last thing I felt like doing with the devil. By refusing, however, I had revealed my cards: he knew that I knew, and that was to his advantage. He knew my weaknesses, my fears, he knew that his name—Fox—had hit me like a punch in the stomach. But he also knew that I could always counter him with a splash of holy water. For the moment, therefore, a temporary truce was established.

I don't think any of those present had noticed our private hostility. Burgomaster Keller seemed to be melting like a candle under its own flame, while the pastor struggled to open the glass cabinet where the Vin Santo was kept on hand for grand occasions. Meanwhile, the housekeeper, her cheeks spotted red with emotion, was looking in vain for a space where she could set down the tray with the Bohemian crystal glasses. And at this point those characteristic features that, to an attentive eye, make him recognizable began to manifest themselves in him (in the devil, I mean): everything about his person reeks of excess, his laugh is raucous, his gestures theatrical, his hair, slicked back and rather long and greasy, is dyed black; his lips are purple and thin, the corners turned up to mimic a perennial smile; his large incisors, shaped like scalpels, are affected by a noticeable diastema; and the voice, that voice, which seems to hold the secret of his charm, is sonorous, trained, with no irregularities or peaks—though if the frequency were slowed down using a magnetic tape, it would reveal a background of sighs and moans. By now it is obvious that the burgomaster and pastor are in his clutches, and that even the housekeeper would dance naked in the middle of the square, if only he asked her. A spectacle, embarrassing to say the least, is taking place before my very eyes, which, like it or not, I am forced to watch. It is incomprehensible how people who are more than mature—the burgomaster, too, is by far over seventy—can behave like children lured by a stick of candy. The parish priest in particular is unable to conceal his excitement over such a presence who has come from afar. A publisher! Who is already taking an interest in his work! "You see, you see?" he says pointing to the various folders that by this time clutter every surface. "A project that has occupied me for twenty years," he continues with a tremor in his voice. "I see, I see," the devil replies, picking up a file and leafing through it with secret rapture. He thumbs through the pages, contemplates them, sinks his nose in them as if searching for the trace of a mysterious aroma, and all this under the well-disposed gaze of the pastor, who doesn't bat an eye—the same man who is usually so possessive about his writings—but on the contrary is pleased that someone has his hands on them. Of course this is not any ordinary person, but a publisher, and from Lucerne on top of it.

"I see, I see," the devil continues. "A laborious effort, an entire life at the service of a community: a work that cannot remain shut away in a drawer, but must take flight." Then, turning to the burgomaster: "And with this there are two, two manuscripts to be sent to the press."

Ah, this is news to me, *tu quoque*, you too, burgomaster, have a novel in the drawer! Who would ever have imagined it? The burgomaster, as visibly confused as a shrinking violet, speaks up: "There's no comparison. Mine is nothing more than a small collection of thoughts, expressed in verse, I wouldn't even remotely dare to call them poems, they are simply a hymn to our mountains."

"Now, now, Herr Burgomaster, don't be so modest. Owing to my long experience I can recognize talent where it lies hidden."

At those words the burgomaster is completely bewildered, and no longer knows what to say. In an attempt to change the subject, he addresses the pastor, and consequently me as well:

"Let me inform you, if I may, of the grandiose project that Dr. Bernhard Fuchs, from Lucerne, has in mind to realize right here in Dichtersruhe. Please, continue, Dr. Fuchs ..."

Dr. Fuchs waves the notebook he is holding as if it were the draft of a political manifesto, and in fact what he is about to say is tantamount to the declaration of a revolution.

"Dichtersruhe does not deserve oblivion," he begins. "Goethe, the distinguished poet, whose magnificent poem was inspired by one of my illustrious ancestors, did not pass through this village fruitlessly. And I, as a custodian of human knowledge and eminent publisher, will not allow that to happen. I will do all I can to see that talent is brought to light, that the chaff is blown away and only the mature wheat remains, and that the sludge is rinsed clean, allowing the nuggets to shine ..."

What an odd way of speaking, I think. Where does this fellow come from? From another era perhaps, whose art of oratory is still stuck to him? Immediately afterwards I realize that eloquence is part of the devil's histrionic nature: the theatrical gestures, bombastic voice, elaborate use of adjectives, the intent look, always ready to seize upon any sign of disbelief in his impromptu audience so he can nip it in the bud. An eminent publisher ... I'd like to see that! Deep in thought, I missed part of his speech, but now he was getting to the point:

"And for this noble reason it is my intention to establish myself in this location, so that it will be easier for me to perform the task of selection and maieutics, which promises to be long and meticulous."

An interminable silence follows. All four of us—even the housekeeper, whom no one has bothered to dismiss—stand before him speechless and dumbfounded. The first to react is the parish priest.

"Do you mean, Dr. Fuchs, that you would do us the honor of establishing a division of your publishing house in our community?"

The devil nods. As much as his power lies in his words, he is well aware that at the right moment even a pause can have its due effect.

And in that prolonged silence I seem to hear the pastor's thoughts, along with those of the burgomaster, grow, as inaudibly as I imagine the growing of grass is, or the budding of leaves on the trees.

The pastor clears his throat, all his enthusiasm suddenly quelled, and his face sags, the nose having turned from red to livid purple.

"I'm afraid," he says, with a tremor in his voice, "that our little community is not suitable for such an ambitious project."

"Why ever not?" the devil presses him, visibly put out.

"Don't misunderstand me, please," the pastor replies. "You do us a great honor to want to establish yourself in our community, but you've caught us unprepared, and above all lacking. In the entire village there is unfortunately not a single vacant building that can feasibly be used to accommodate a publishing house ..." And so saying he glances sadly at his papers. He can already see his dream vanishing: the three volumes bound in red Moroccan leather with gold letters—that's how he imagines his printed memoirs—go back to being a pile of yellowed sheets, scattered here and there around the study. But the burgomaster speaks up.

"However ..."

"However?" the pastor echoes him, with a shred of hope.

"There's the old mill."

"But it's uninhabitable."

"The plan for its restoration has been ready at Town Hall for three years. I would simply have to call a special council meeting to speed up the process."

"But it will still take time."

"Less than you might think. Besides that, there is another pending project that concerns the former Ursuline convent. The only reason the work hasn't been started yet is because up until now we didn't know what it could be used for. But now there is no doubt, those historical walls could not be put to better use.

"But of course," the pastor exclaims, "I don't know why I didn't think of it!" He is suddenly cocky again, and his nose has once more turned red as a beacon. Nonetheless, he continues to have a trace of doubt.

"It will take time to restore the building, however, whereas I imagine that Dr. Fuchs needs an immediate accommodation in order to begin his work of selection."

"That's true," the burgomaster confirms. "To begin the work and complete it will take at least six months, but in the meantime we could make some space in Town Hall available, an area that is currently used as an archive. It would be two rooms. Would that be adequate, Dr. Fuchs?"

Dr. Fuchs, the devil in person, thinks that for the time being that would suffice to collect and store the material to be reviewed. From the expression on his face, however, he does not seem entirely satisfied. Still, it only takes a few minutes for everything to be arranged.

To this day, thinking about it, I can't understand how the negotiation had turned out to the devil's full advantage. I was forced to witness, helplessly, a diabolical fraud. The very individuals—the pastor and the burgomaster—who had always protected Dichtersruhe from the intrusion of outsiders looking to settle there, those very same individuals were now rolling out the red carpet for this stranger, with only the vaguest hope of seeing their writings published. Chapeau!

The result of that meeting was that the burgomaster would grant the devil use of two large rooms in Town Hall, fully furnished; and for his personal lodgings, the pastor, in a fit of generosity, offered to make available, for a token sum, a house that he owned, which he rented each summer to a family from Berlin.

During the meeting I hadn't said a word and only at the end was I asked for my opinion. What I wouldn't have done or said at that moment to rouse them from the spell! But all that came out of my mouth was a laconic "Splendid." Then I added something more, but I would have done better to keep my mouth shut.

"And why not establish a literary award as well?"

I wish I'd never said it! I meant it to be merely an ironic quip, and instead it was greeted with great enthusiasm.

"A literary award named after Goethe. A wonderful idea!" the pastor exclaimed. And so, without intending to, I too had contributed to the ignoble farce.

When it came time for farewells, the devil, alias Bernhard Fuchs, fixed me with those murky-yellow eyes in which cunning and deference seemed to be at odds, and addressed me with a vaguely mocking grin:

"Perhaps you too, Father Cornelius, have written a novel. Don't hesitate to take it out of the drawer."

"I don't believe I have one."

"Are you really sure, positively certain about that?"

"Absolutely certain."

"You never know, there may be something that you have

forgotten. Who knows, maybe some letters. Or a secret diary ..."

At that moment I didn't give much weight to his words, but they would come back to me later on.

The devil took his leave, promising to return soon, after we'd had time to arrange things. He got into an old Daimler, complete with chauffeur, and left the village.

8

After the devil's departure, the pastor, the burgomaster, and I met several times to discuss the details of this ... folly, which could not be described as anything else. I tried to get them to think about what they were about to do. Did anyone remember the name of the publishing house by any chance? Did we have an address we could confirm? A basis on which to verify the reliability of that individual more thoroughly? But there was no chance of making them use their heads. I don't think they even remembered the man's features. On the other hand, if I'd had to give a description of him, even I would have found it difficult, though I had observed him closely. In my memory, his figure fragmented into various garish details, like his lurid corpulence, or the affected sound of his consummate actor's voice. On these we all agreed, but someone had also noticed his limp, which led one to think he had an artificial leg; and didn't that inky-black hair look like a wig?

Every attempt on my part to induce them to be more cautious in completely trusting an individual whom they knew nothing about failed. I wonder how they would have reacted knowing that they had just made a contract with the devil himself.

Refusing to listen to me, the burgomaster immediately convened a council meeting, and within a few days the two rooms on the second floor of Town Hall were emptied out; the archive's hundreds of folders found a new home in the basement. The walls were repainted, the marble floors polished to a mirror sheen, and the rooms furnished with drop-leaf chests of drawers and massive walnut desks. Not only that, but the burgomaster insisted on launching the literary award right away. There was no doubt as to what to name it, but there were several heated discussions regarding the limits to be imposed on the competition: indeed, no one wanted to open it to the entire national territory. In the end it was decided that only authors residing in our canton would be eligible for the Goethe award. The call for entries was printed as soon as possible, with a rather tight deadline, thus giving Dichtersruhe's writers the chance to submit their manuscripts in the prescribed time, while at the same time trying to exclude all the others. Xenophobia still reigned, except toward the devil, of course.

Partly due to bad weather, I stayed indoors in the days that followed. The Föhn, the warm deadly wind, swept the valley for two days, depressing people's spirits and prompting suicide.

During that solitary time I recalled the malevolent allusion that had been made to me by Dr. Sly Fox regarding an alleged diary that I kept at the bottom of a drawer, and which I had perhaps forgotten. Could the devil know something specific about me, or had he perhaps hit the bull's eye accidentally? It was precisely because of a diary, in fact, that I found myself sequestered here: a notebook found in the room of a young seminarian, my student, who had died in mysterious circumstances. His name was Stefan. It is true that I had become the spiritual father of that boy who, left alone in the world, had grown attached to me in a morbid way, but I had always kept the proper distance, thinking only of the good of his soul. It is equally true that his death had occurred just after a heated discussion on faith, and that on that occasion he had expressed his wish to leave this world: words to which I had not given much weight. The tragedy occurred during an excursion in the mountains, along an easy trail that posed no great risks. We'd left early in the morning, bound for a shelter at an altitude high above, but halfway there, given the approach of a storm, our guide had decided to turn back. Only upon our return did we notice the boy's absence; it was already dark and we were not equipped to start searching for him. We hoped that Stefan had been able to find his way down on his own. Although it was the middle of summer, the nighttime temperature dropped quite a bit, but we were consoled by the fact that there was a sleeping bag in his backpack, capable of providing protection from the cold. The search began the following day at first light, and went on until evening, with no success. The next day the area was scoured inch by inch, with the help of alpine rescue dogs as well. The hope that the boy might still be alive gradually began to shrink. Until finally his body was found at the bottom of a ravine. When I was asked to identify him, I nearly passed out: the whole right side of the handsome face I knew had been mangled, the flesh ripped off by foxes, by the abominable foxes.

Everything led one to believe that it was a tragic accident: Stefan, unaware of the fact that the group was turning back, had continued along the trail, until he'd been caught by the impending storm. This would have been the most plausible version of events if a diary had not been found in his room, in which he openly expressed his spiritual torments. And the fact that my name was also found in those pages gave rise to a series of suspicions and rumors about me. Rumors that showed no sign of letting up, but continued to be fomented by those who wanted to steal the coveted philosophy post from me. Suspicions of who knows what kind of vile relations between me and my pupil began to spread, and some even implied that I was the one who drove him to suicide. Until the bishop, to silence the scandal, assigned me to the parish of Dichtersruhe as vicar. Obviously, everything was hushed up: the death of the young seminarian was attributed to an accident. The diary and its contents remained classified, in the bishop's hands, and after my departure everything returned to normal. The devil's allusion, therefore, could only be the result of diabolical intuition. Yet it proved to be a pointed gibe aimed at my conscience. That was exactly how the devil's tactics worked: fire a barb at random until you strike someone's guilty conscience. And my conscience was not entirely clean. That face torn to shreds by foxes continued to appear in my dreams. I saw his body fall, flailing in the air in a vain swimming motion. I didn't give myself a moment's peace, in fact, for not having understood how grave my pupil's situation was, and to have left him prey to his doubts and fears just when he needed me most. But only I knew that.

My state of isolation lasted two days, until one evening the parish priest invited me to have supper with him. The thought of having to spend the whole evening with that boring old man would not have enticed me if it had not been for the fact that it was a good opportunity to try to offer him a warning. I found him unusually cheerful and well disposed toward me, and the supper prepared by the housekeeper was also excellent. For the occasion, the pastor uncorked a bottle of fine wine, Château de Praz, chosen from his well-stocked cellar, and at the end of the meal he lit a cigar. He took me to his study, which had been tidied up, and showed me all his writings reorganized and collected in various folders complete with dates. Thinking it was the right time to instill some doubt in him regarding the figure of Dr. Fuchs, I tried to lead up to the subject in a roundabout way and asked him what he thought of the strange phenomenon of the foxes who had even ventured so far as the village.

"It's a natural phenomenon," he said, frowning a little. "As you can see, the threat has been eliminated."

"Rather I would say that it stopped spontaneously. Don't you find it strange?"

"It was certainly our prayers that drove them away."

"Do you remember a similar phenomenon occurring at any time in the past?"

"No, if my memory serves me, we have never had anything like this."

"What if their presence was a divine intervention, a kind of warning?"

The pastor let his cigar ash drop to the floor. He gave me a bewildered look.

"A warning of what?"

"Of the approach of a calamity in our village."

"What calamity are you referring to?"

"Doesn't it seem strange to you that soon afterwards that peculiar individual showed up in the village?"

"Who are you talking about?"

"About Dr. Fuchs."

"And you think Dr. Fuchs is a bearer of evil?"

The pastor erupted in unrestrained laughter that resulted in a series of phlegmy coughs. When he'd recovered, he tossed his cigar into the fireplace.

"My dear Cornelius, you are delirious. Don't you realize, on the contrary, what good fortune we've had? When has an important publisher ever been so kind as to personally take an interest in us? As for foxes and rabies, forget about them, otherwise you will only fuel superstition."

Our conversation ended there. The pastor, however, had invited me to supper to assign me a task that lay outside his usual pastoral duties. I was to take a first look at the manuscripts, which had already begun to arrive in large numbers at Town Hall. It was a matter of making a first cut, perhaps accompanied by a brief comment: a screening process, easily done. "After all," he said, "you were a teacher at the seminary for a long time, and you are certainly competent for such a task. Think of them as compositions written by your students."

I did not at all like his allusion to the seminary and to my students. Although, perhaps I was becoming paranoid.

The following morning the town messenger brought a dozen manuscripts to me at the rectory—as many as he could carry. I spread them out on my desk, subdividing them according to how thick they were. I would of course start with the slimmer ones. To begin with, the writing could give me a first impression of the author. Most were handwritten, some in block letters, and only a few were typed, on some old Olivetti with encrusted characters. Though I would have expected fictional works, I found myself instead faced with concrete facts, complete with names and dates. As for the judgment, albeit brief, that I was supposed to express, I had to assess each one appropriately, case by case, and I knew I had to act with caution. Skimming through those pages I quickly realized that I held in my hands what until then had been denied to me, that is, the chance to delve more deeply into the minds of my parishioners. You couldn't expect much from individuals who'd been born and still lived in such a tiny region on the fringes of history. Many of the accounts referred to family occurrences told with great sincerity, and at times with too much candor. It was strange that people who were so reserved and reticent, even toward their confessor, were willing to disclose their secrets provided there was a chance they would see them in print. A great many skeletons came out of closets, were taken by the hand and made to perform in a shambling danse macabre. Though initially I had accepted the task unwillingly, the assignment was now starting to get interesting.

The next day the messenger brought me just as many manuscripts, then even more and others still. By that time I was completely occupied by a charge that was becoming more and more onerous. I got up early in the morning and went to bed at night with my eyes burning; I had strange dreams, owing to the countless stories I read. Grotesque characters paraded before my eyes, one after the other. Dichtersruhe in my dreams became a huge stage lit by bonfires, and the actors went up to the platform one by one to perform their roles, while all around, in the darkness of the forest, the eyes of lurking foxes glinted in the fire's light. One night I dreamt that I was traveling by train. I was sitting by the window, my gaze lost in the snowy expanse, and I soon found out that what I was seeing wasn't snow, but scraps of paper: there were mountains of pages, folios, crumbling manuscripts, torn sheets that covered every inch of ground. And running alongside the train, on this whitish surface, was a fox, slavering from his gaping jaws. I woke up with a start and found myself sitting on the bed, trembling, while from outside I could hear the foxes baying, as clearly as if they were in the room. Anyone who has never heard it can't understand what it's like: no other animal's cry so closely mimics a human shriek. It was three o'clock in the morning, surely the villagers must be fretful, but I had only to look out the window to see that not a single light had been lit in the entire village. At that moment a terrifying thought crossed my mind: was it possible that I was the only one hearing those howls? That they were only in my head, like a message directed solely at me, that meant to say, "I'll be back, just you wait!"

9

The following day, right on time, the devil returned to Dichtersruhe, aboard his black Daimler, the sedan with its darkened windows that was his habitual means of getting around. Where it was kept, nobody knew; just as no one could explain how it was always ready and waiting when needed, as if the devil and his driver shared a telepathic bond. Undoubtedly there was also a telephone in the house rented to him by the parish priest, which swept away any fanciful hypotheses.

Welcomed by the town delegation, he was first led to see the rooms prepared for him, and was flattered and fawned over by the burgomaster who followed him around like a puppy dog. The burgomaster insisted on inaugurating the new venue with a ribbon-cutting ceremony and a short speech. As an exception, the parish priest was also present, invited to give the blessing. But liturgical rites were not to the devil's liking, and with a skillful move he sidestepped the divine intrusion; nor did the pastor have the courage to insist, since the publisher had already started speaking, informing us that a prominent bank would subsidize the prize to the tune of ten thousand francs. This news was followed by a murmur of wonder, and even applause. When it comes to money, everything else takes a back seat. Dr. Fuchs expressed his satisfaction with the premises, asking only that curtains be hung at the windows, since he suffered from hypersensitivity to light. From there we moved on to the house that had been made available for his private use. The pastor accompanied him on a tour through the inside. As the devil climbed the stairs to reach the upper floor, I realized that he had some difficulty bending his left leg, which was visibly affected by an unusual rigidity. I thus confirmed that he had an artificial limb. After inspecting the rooms, *le diable boiteux* asked if he might remove a whole collection of miniature holy-water fonts from a wall, with the excuse that he had to find a place for a piece of furniture of which he was particularly fond. And finally, since the house was not far from the church, he obtained the pastor's promise to minimize the use of the bells, because, as he put it, he suffered from an unusual malformation of the eardrum, which made certain acute sounds unbearably painful to him. Whatever the devil might have asked him—even if it meant tearing down the church overnight—the pastor would gladly have consented to it.

Dr. Bernhard Fuchs settled into the house that the pastor had made available to him and soon enough could be seen ambling around the village, followed by looks of admiration and curiosity. In the morning one might meet him walking down the street or at the café Oetker, which had quickly become his headquarters. He was always surrounded by throngs of admirers who accompanied him everywhere. He was a master at billiards, and also at the card game, Jass, but heaven help the unfortunate game partner who did not prove to be at his level. Sometimes he dined at the Pension Müller, other times he had supper at the Weberns, more rarely at the Meyers, whose cooking he didn't particularly care for. Wherever he went, he seemed to enjoy unlimited credit. As soon as he set foot in a pub, he always found someone ready to pull out his wallet on behalf of him. In return the publisher lavishly handed out Maria Mancini cigars, packaged—to hear him tell it— specifically to promote the imminent publication of *The Magic Mountain*. Given these beginnings, his social ascent was very swift: the agricultural bank gave him an unlimited line of credit, and the Lions Club welcomed him as an honorary member.

After settling into the offices provided to him in Town Hall, the first thing he wanted to know was how many entries had been received up to then; he also demanded a complete list of the applicants. The town messenger came to pick up the manuscripts that I had sifted through, bringing me others in turn.

"Dr. Fuchs would like to have detailed synopses of the contents," the clerk said as he handed them over to me.

What incredible nerve!

"Oh really? You can tell him to write his own synopses."

The situation was paradoxical: albeit indirectly, I was working for the devil. He was indeed exploiting his position of preeminence, issuing orders, so as to gain strength to the extent that I weakened. The others were now puppets in his hands, while I was the last obstacle to be overcome before he would have free rein over all of

Dichtersruhe. Accordingly—as I well knew—he was prepared to act with great determination. What scared me
the most was the fact that there wasn't a single person in
the whole village willing to support me. Judging by the
reverence with which he'd been received, I had by then
dismissed the possibility of finding an ally. Everyone
doted on him, and there wasn't a day when baskets of
fresh vegetables, salamis, cheeses, and cases of beer did
not arrive at his door. The only one in a position to help
me was the pastor, a man of the church and of experience, but he had already made his stance clear, defending
the publisher and forbidding me to defame someone he
considered to be a benefactor. It was obvious that any
further attempt to caution the pastor would compromise
my situation even more. Stirred up for good reason, in
his eyes I was now a deranged lunatic. I had confirmation
of it one evening when the pastor invited the devil to
dinner.

The walls of the rectory were quite thick and did not
allow any sound to filter through. There was, however, a
spot in the inner courtyard that was just below the pastor's dining room, and from there one could hear their
voices coming from a window that had been left open on
that rather warm evening.

I am not ashamed to say that I stationed myself there to
be able to eavesdrop. At first I heard only uproarious
laughter from the devil, then I began to make out his
voice. He seemed to be the only one talking; from the
place where I stood I could hear him clearly, though I
found it somewhat difficult to understand the meaning of
the words. All of a sudden I had the feeling that he was
talking about me. Words like seminary, disgrace, suicide
... they could only refer to my past and to the tragedy that

still weighed heavily on my conscience. His voice came and went, a sign that he was pacing up and down the room. The words became more comprehensible only when he approached the balcony, leaning out to look below. I flattened myself against the wall to avoid being discovered. "He could become a danger to the community," he said. "He should be removed and made to undergo psychiatric treatment."

He pronounced that sentence loudly, as if he knew that I was able to hear him. Then he shut the window, and I couldn't hear anything more of their conversation.

Meanwhile in Dichtersruhe, the Goethe award was on everyone's lips. There was talk of nothing else. Ten thousand Swiss francs was a handsome sum. Generally, a writer settles for a fake gold plaque and the applause of a scanty audience. But when money is associated with glory ... It was only a few days before everyone in the village knew about it. The Goethe award was becoming the most coveted prize in all of Switzerland: not only was there a nice stash to pocket, but also the promise of seeing one's book published in a very prestigious series; the imprint reserved for the great names of German-language literature no less.

But did this prestigious imprint really exist? Did the publishing house really exist? I wondered if anyone had ever bothered to look into it, but evidently no one had deemed it necessary.

Without realizing it, the inhabitants of Dichtersruhe were losing their heads. When they found out that I was responsible for the first screening of the manuscripts we'd received, they began to besiege me. They stopped me on the street or showed up at the door with some excuse or other, so they could influence my selection in favor of a son, a brother, a relative ... Never as at that time had the church been lit by so many candles, never before had the collection boxes overflowed with offerings of silver coins. Even in the privacy of the confessional they gave it a try. They did not come straight to the point, but circled around it as if it were a plate of hot soup. There was always someone who was interceding for someone else, and it always involved salvation of the soul, conversion, and repentance. As if great literature were the work of pious people, motivated by good intentions. Quite the contrary. Nonetheless, people often confuse literary talent with moral integrity. They are inclined to measure their own lives by the criterion of the most banal literature, that which exalts positive values, in which everything is resolved for the collective good, wherein the wicked lose and the good triumph. But if it was all so simple I wouldn't be here telling this story.

My hopes were fruitless. Of all the manuscripts that I had read up to then, in that deluge of useless and redundant pages, there was nothing, in my opinion, that was worthy of mention. In rejecting them, I should have assigned each of them a penance, written at the bottom of the last page. *Tear up the pages of your manuscript one by one*—is what I should have told them—*rewrite it ten times, eliminate at least a dozen adjectives on each page, take your wasted paper and toss it in the fire.* And what penance should I have assigned to the so-called poets who were convinced that to produce verse all they had to do was start a new line? During the lengthy hours devoted to the first screening of the manuscripts, I seem to have discovered a fundamental principle that could be applied to practically all the arts, and to literature in particular, which could be formulated as follows: *The greater the number of people who dedicate themselves to the same creative activity, the more that activity declines.* Or perhaps, reversing the terms of the proposition: *The more an art declines, the greater the number of people who dedicate themselves to it.* But this is a sign of our times. By now great literature ends up being measured by babbling street chatter, the purer voices drowned out like a child's song in the din of a local market. The cause of all this is fear of indifference. Heaven help you if you are judged unworthy of others' attention. Better to be accused, slandered, mocked, rather than ignored. What induces people to write, if not the vague dread of not having done enough to ensure that they live on? For that reason we must prove ourselves, circulate our name, our image, be reflected in the eyes of others and, from there, indelibly engrave ourselves on the metaphysical plate of the universe, thus enabling the Almighty to put the pieces of the Erector Set back together on Resurrection Day. All of humanity nourishes this foolish hope. And the word is the ideal medium. If at the beginning of creation there was the word, is it not possible that life and the universe were created for the sole purpose of being able to write about them?

10

A black cloud continued to loom over Dichtersruhe, as black as the ink poured over hundreds and thousands of pages that no one would ever read. No matter how long my work of selection went on, the task appeared more and more onerous. By my calculation, a year would not be enough for me to be able to thoroughly review all the entries. I spoke to the burgomaster about it, and he presented me with another problem: the difficulty of impaneling a neutral jury, that is, of finding individuals who were completely uninvolved with the competition. Taking into account the close family ties among the inhabitants of Dichtersruhe, only the unmarried burgomaster Keller was left to give me a hand; though he too had a book in the drawer, he could not participate in the contest. Lastly, there was cantonal councilor Linz, who was one of the few in the village whose fingers were not ink-stained. But even so, the problem was only partly solved: to get through all that material in the allocated time would require at least a dozen capable and willing helpers.

The prospect of having to postpone everything until the

following year would have upset more than a few people. There was also the risk that, after a year, the bank financially supporting the prize might no longer see its way to granting such a striking sum and might reduce it or even eliminate it from its budget.

The burgomaster convened a special meeting in the town hall council chamber, which Dr. Fuchs, naturally, attended. The conclusion was that the prize could not be postponed, that the news had already been circulated to the press, and that the announcement of the competition had also been issued and was posted in plain sight on the bulletin boards of every town in the canton. It was not a peaceable meeting; some individuals proposed their own solutions that inevitably conflicted with those of others. There were those who recommended reading only the works that had been submitted first—the postmark would attest to the date. Others suggested choosing only the shorter works, or perhaps excluding memoirs, or, why not consider only poetry collections?

The final word belonged to the devil.

"In my long experience as a publisher," he said, with his usual pomposity, "thousands of manuscripts have crossed my desk. Goethe used to say that he did not even need to open a book to judge its quality: he merely had to smell it. I have not come quite that far, but I can assure you that I need only read about twenty pages, sometimes even less, to know what a work is like. Therefore I suggest that our vicar and his assistants adopt this technique. In addition, to lend a hand to him and to any others who would like to take on this task, I will send for a person with experience in this area, to coordinate the effort."

At the end of the session a compromise was reached: only the easily legible works, typewritten if possible,

would be reviewed—even if that favored the more afflu-
ent class. Moreover, all those that from the first few pages
revealed a poor command of the language, or contained
syntax and spelling errors, were to be rejected. That same
evening a reading committee was formed which, in addition to the burgomaster and cantonal councilor Linz, was
also joined by the archivist and the secretary, both ineli-
gible to enter the competition. We agreed that all rejected
manuscripts would be returned, with a cover letter that in
any case should be gentle and encouraging.

When the special session concluded, we all went to the
café Oetker to end the evening fittingly, as usual, with a
mug of beer. As we took our places at the table, the devil
and I found ourselves facing one another. I hadn't seen
him at such close quarters since our first meeting in the
pastor's study. It seemed to me that he had gained considerable weight; his satin waistcoat was about to burst.
Surely he fed on souls, but he was also undeniably a big
guzzler. I noticed that he appeared uncomfortable: I don't
know whether it was due to my person or to the crucifix I
wore on my chest. The fact is that I considered it to be the
right moment to openly confront him.

"Dr. Fuchs," I said firmly, "when will we have the opportunity to see at least one volume from your prestigious
series? We would like to know the name of one of the titles
at least, or if nothing else, we would be satisfied if you
would tell us the name of your publishing house in
Lucerne."

By way of response he displayed a set of teeth reminis-
cent of the battlements of a turret:

"All in due course, my dear Father Cornelius," he said in
a dulcet tone. "Here and now is not the time to bore you all
with complicated administrative and financial matters."

So saying, he thought he had silenced me, but when I least expected it, the burgomaster himself backed me up.

"It would be nice," he intervened timidly, "to have at least some idea of how the books that you intend to publish will look." And then cantonal councilor Linz, who was also the president of the agricultural bank, came forward to press him on another front.

"Regarding the sum of ten thousand francs, perhaps it would be appropriate to deposit it in an account opened in the name of the Goethe award, don't you think?"

At those words Dr. Fuchs squirmed in his seat, causing the chair to creak. Was it only my impression, or had a small wart on his nose actually erupted in those few moments?

"The publishing house I represent has published all the German classics, including Goethe, of course. However, as it only recently decided to turn its attention to contemporary literature, our designers are still developing an eye-catching, modern-style cover, and as soon as it is ready, you will be the first to see it. As for the award sum, for the moment we must be content with a promise—one made to me, however, by a trustworthy individual. As soon as I receive the check, I will be sure to deposit it in your bank."

Hearing him talk about promises, I couldn't suppress a hearty snicker, which had an entirely unexpected effect. Perhaps at that moment the devil wanted to pretend he hadn't heard it and, to appear composed, tilted his chair backwards, leaning heavily against the seat back. Sturdy as the chair was, it did not hold up and collapsed under his weight. His body arched like a harpooned whale and, in a vain attempt to rescue himself, the devil clutched at the tablecloth, dragging a whole array of silverware, dishes, and glasses along with him.

There is nothing like a ruinous fall to provoke hilarity in those who observe the incident: although the unfortunate victim may have suffered serious injury, the laughter is irrepressible and contagious. Several customers, the waiter and the café owner rushed to the devil's aid, making a huge effort to hoist him up on his feet after freeing him from the clutches of the arm rests that gripped his posterior like crab claws. Nothing broken, a side-piece of his eyeglasses had been bent, his jacket had a vertical split seam on the back, but otherwise everything seemed fine. As he accompanied him to the door, the café owner assured him that there was no need to worry about the damage that had been done, while the waiter, with a whisk broom he'd found somewhere, continued brushing his back like a barber's apprentice.

Once the door had closed behind him, the whole place seemed to hover in an unreal silence. The only thing that could be clearly heard was the clinking of earthenware shards and glass fragments that a scullery maid was sweeping up from the floor. No one at our table dared to say a word either. Until cantonal councilor Linz spoke up.

"Let's hope that this incident will not have repercussions on the prize."

When all's said and done, the councilor was not wrong. The devil can't stand being laughed at, that is his weak point, and for certain he would avenge himself. Already that same night, as I was returning home, I had the feeling that someone was following me. I paid no attention to it, but when I was near the rectory, in the cone of light cast by a streetlamp, I saw clearly the silhouette of a fox crossing the street.

11

To further disrupt a situation already in itself confused, a few days later, as had been announced, the person who was to assist us in selecting the manuscripts that would participate in the competition arrived promptly from Lucerne. The usual black car, driven by a chauffeur whose face no one had yet seen, delivered her.

We were somewhat nonplussed to see a petulant woman in her fifties, with a hooked owlish nose, getting out of the car. Of all the shades of red available, nature seemed to have chosen the worst rust imaginable for her hair and the worst tone for her complexion, which, lacking transparency, appeared pasty and opaque, dotted with blackish bristles like a piece of boiled pork rind. Dr. Fuchs introduced her as a close colleague: "the editor", the individual who was able to decree the life or death of an unpublished novel. A cordial antipathy instantly arose between the two of us. To begin with, she started criticizing my work, accusing me of having formed too hasty and superficial a judgment on several manuscripts which, in her opinion, deserved greater consideration. Consequently, most of the writings that I had dismissed with the words "negative," "impractical," or "less than mediocre," were returned to my desk so that I might reformulate my assessment; which I refused to do, sending them back to her with one word: "reconfirmed," "reconfirmed," "reconfirmed". It was two weeks of hell. Not a day passed without furious discussions exploding between us. I don't know how many times I saw her charge into my study waving a manuscript and insulting me for not having grasped the (oh, so deeply!) hidden potentialities of some promising young author's text. After a while she didn't even speak to me, she simply tossed a manuscript on my desk, then turned on her heels and left without a word. I wondered what smoky German beer hall the devil had recruited her in: with those brawny, hirsute calves, that sallow skin poking out from the cork-wedge sandals, I imagined her capable of carrying a dozen or so liter mugs of beer, though substantially incapable of being moved by the beauty of a verse.

Things had not gone any better for the others either: the burgomaster could not resign himself to being treated so rudely, and councilor Linz had actually had a nervous breakdown. Fortunately for us, after two weeks of harassment, that repugnant creature got into the predictable black sedan and went on her way to Lucerne, or perhaps to hell. Of the hundreds of manuscripts we received, most were set aside to be returned to the senders. It took some time for the clerk responsible for the task to finish putting them in envelopes, complete with a personalized letter. The person assigned to return the rejected entries would not find it easy, having to face the author's wrath. In fact, the first troubles started as soon as redelivery of the eliminated works began. Although the old adage ensures immunity to the bearer of a letter, regardless of its content, the category of messenger has always been unpopular. And matters did not improve when, to save on postage, the task of returning the works declined by the committee was entrusted to a newly hired boy, who often found himself in serious difficulty. The procedure called for the recipient of any document to affix his signature in order to attest to its receipt. Enough time for the poor innocent messenger to have all kinds of abuse heaped on him.

As soon as the first manuscripts found their way home, an unspoken madness began to spread through the village. And this madness was infecting eminent individuals. At the café Oetker heated discussions, if not actual brawls, often broke out; there were those who could not accept the fact that they had been excluded, while others, not having yet received a response, gloated in the hope of lasting to the end, and even if they didn't win first prize maybe they would at least deserve a mention. Soon enough, the whole village split into two camps: the rejected and the chosen, or rather, the disappointed and the hopeful. Relations between people who until then had never had a reason to clash began to be strained, and this happened especially among the leading figures of the village. It seemed that a first furious altercation had occurred between Dr. Meyer, the district physician, and the elementary school teacher Webern. The two had been friends since childhood, they and their wives saw each other constantly, and for years now they'd been in the habit of challenging each other at chess every Saturday afternoon at the café Oetker. When they missed their usual Saturday appointment for the first time, their friends were worried, but neither of the two would give an explanation. Apparently the two men had argued violently. A bystander who had witnessed the scene claimed that the teacher, Webern, had knocked Dr. Meyer's hat off his head, and also verbally attacked him with a distinctly uttered "scribbler," to which Dr. Meyer had replied with "pen pusher." Another such instance arose between town councilor Müller and the archivist Schwartz. What had been kept within the limits of a heated altercation between the two men evolved into a sequel on the part of their respective wives who, having run into each other at the market, had savagely come to blows, resulting in both of them rolling under the fruit stand. Episodes of this kind were multiplying day by day. The animosity of those rejected escalated and, if at first everyone was against everyone else, now there were two clearly distinct camps, and as with an hourglass, while one glass bulb filled up, the other drained.

12

Dr. Fuchs made additional nighttime visits to the parish priest. I would waste no time finding out what they were up to; at the time I could only suspect it, but undoubtedly, each time he came, the devil was tightening his net around the unfortunate victim. For certain he continued to foster that poor old man's illusion of being able to publish his memoirs, so that in return he could obtain—as I would soon discover—the legal usufruct to the house that he had moved into. He would arrive late at night. I could hear him heavily climb the stairs leading up to the first floor and then come back down a few hours later. From the window I could see his figure headed toward the black sedan that was waiting for him across the road. The last time he left later than usual. The light in the pastor's study remained on for some time longer: from my bed I could see it reflected in the curve of the metal eaves. Around two a.m. I fell asleep, but I was immediately awakened by the excited ringing of the bell that the pastor used to summon the housekeeper. It was she, in fact, who knocked at my door a few minutes later. Disheveled, and with a coat thrown over her nightgown, she looked distraught. "Father is dying," she kept shouting. I raced up the stairs, but I was not in time to enter his study before the pastor had already expired. Slumped against the back of his favorite armchair, the one where he had spent thousands of hours writing his memoirs, Father Cristoforo, his hands clawing at the armrests, wore a horrible grimace. His eyes were wide open, and so was his mouth, minus his dentures, which in the violent throes of death had shot out over the desk and rolled onto the carpet. There wasn't a trace of his documents: a single blank sheet of paper lay on the clear surface of his desk, suggesting his intent to write a letter to an unknown recipient.

The whole village attended the funeral. I performed the funeral rites as interim parish priest; though on the one hand I hoped to be acting pastor only for the time it would take to be transferred elsewhere, on the other hand I felt that I could not leave my flock at the mercy of that demon. He too attended the ceremony, the devil that is, but he kept to himself for the duration of the service. Only at the end, when those present filed past the open grave to toss in a clod of earth, only then did the devil get in line; when his turn came, he dropped a hefty bundle of papers secured with rubber bands onto the casket. The significance of that gesture may perhaps have escaped those in attendance; some may likely have thought it was a matter of complying with the final wishes of the deceased. It was clear to me, however, that the weighty packet was the work to which Father Cristoforo had devoted himself his entire life, and that he would never ever have wanted to see it buried along with him. An unexpected stroke of luck for Dr. Fuchs, who did not have to pay anything in exchange for what he had obtained.

A few days later, in fact, a notary came to see me. As I had foreseen, the documents in his possession spoke plainly: the devil had obtained the legal right to the house of the deceased for an indefinite period of time. Only a close relative—and there did not appear to be one—could have challenged the bequest, appealing to a presumed lack of understanding and volition on the part of the old pastor, though not without becoming entangled in costly and interminable court proceedings.

By now the devil's strategy was becoming glaringly obvious: as he had acted with the parish priest, so he would defraud others. Proffering the mirage of success, he would one by one strike the more ambitious, prosperous people, obtaining favors from them. And he would not hesitate to discredit a praiseworthy work and plunge its author into the blackest despondency when he did not see a personal gain. By so doing he would corrupt each person's soul, raising altars to the mediocre and digging graves for the deserving; he would thereby drag everyone into a turmoil of hatred, pride, exaltation, and misery. What mattered most was to damn as many souls as possible. And hordes of other devils would flock to his aid, who had until then remained locked in the drawer.

Father Cristoforo's death was able to dampen the general animosity somewhat, but this state of truce did not last long: the rancor of the rejected authors toward those who had made the first cut started growing again. The children of the excluded ones, who were in the majority, formed actual retaliatory gangs against the unfortunate children of the chosen, waiting for them on the street to throw stones at them. And the new town messenger, whose duty it was to return the rejected entries, genuinely risked his life when, riding his bicycle with its parcel carrier overloaded with manuscripts, he was hit by a car that continued on its way without stopping to help. It turned out to be patently clear that the act was premeditated. The matter attracted the attention of the cantonal gendarmerie, which found itself faced with the usual solid wall of silence. Still, the intervention of the authorities helped to re-establish an apparent order at least, if not to soothe some of the more heated souls. Secretly though, the excluded rejects formed a cohesive band that grew ever larger, and seethed, spreading false accusations. In my new capacity as parish priest I would have thought I was *super partes*, but I was wrong. I too, along with the burgomaster and councilor Linz, was accused of favoritism and even charged with having selected certain manuscripts in exchange for money.

13

Meanwhile, tourism languished. Whereas in June there were still some outsiders around, by July and August they had all gone. In fact, you cannot spend your vacation in a place where the shutters are lowered at half-mast, where merchandise is sold at black-market prices, and where, in the rare places still open, the service is awful, the food second-rate, and the staff rude.

Merchants and craftsmen no longer had the slightest desire to earn an honest living, as they had done until then. The local street markets with arts and crafts and food specialties had completely disappeared, and the three renowned inns displayed big signs with discouraging notices such as "closed for restorations," "will reopen in October," or "closed due to change of management." Even family-owned boardinghouses declared "no vacancy," when in reality they were completely empty. As if that weren't enough, large warnings were posted at the entrance to the various scenic trails, advising hikers of the risk they were taking by entering the forest, due to the foxes and the rampant epidemic of wild rabies. People remained shut up in their houses, the village looked as if it had been devastated by the plague, and only the town messenger roamed the streets occasionally—like an angel of death riding a bicycle—to designate the person about to die, that is, yet another rejected author. And there was no way to ward off the sentence: even if you barricaded yourself in the house pretending not to be home, the messenger would soon return with implacable regularity. It is true that the envelope also contained a consoling, encouraging letter, which was supposed to be of comfort, but for some the affront of having been eliminated before others was a dishonor that could only be cleansed with blood. And most often the blood was that of family members. In fact, there were several cases of violence, even serious ones: a woman, hurled down the stairs by her husband, nearly died, and there were at least two cases of suicide. For the others, those who managed to endure the disgrace, there remained the reproach that was punctually displayed when the failed novelist, or misunderstood poet, found himself at the table with his family, when a spouse's obstinate silence became all too eloquent, and the light of all hope seemed to fade away like the bluish flame of a candle about to sputter out.

These family dramas were revealed to me behind the grille of the confessional. My parishioners came to me so that I might release them from the obsession that had taken hold of them. Literature was the work of the devil, or rather, it was his favorite weapon—so they told me. Which I knew all too well.

For my part, I felt more and more responsible for what was happening. In any case, it was essential that the work of selection be completed: it was already the end of August and only one month remained before the awarding of the prize. Each time I finished reading a manuscript, I wondered what the consequences of my decision would be; so, before expressing my opinion, I consulted with the burgomaster and with councilor Linz, whose situations were no better than mine. The problem was that nothing distinctive had yet emerged from all that rubbish. We passed the last manuscripts on to one another with the hope that one of us might find something good in it that had escaped the others, but the judgments unfortunately agreed: the needle on the scale remained fixed at zero. Only one candidate was left, though she could not be put forth: Marta Bauer, whose competing entry was a book of banal nonsense rhymes, illustrated with splendid drawings. But having to award a prize named after Goethe to a little book of children's nursery rhymes risked inciting a popular insurrection. Accordingly we reconvened with the rest of the committee and came to the conclusion that, despite being contrary to the publisher's wishes, it would be better for everyone if the award were postponed to the following year; the hope was that in the meantime some real talent would emerge. To some members of the review committee the decision made without the publisher's knowledge seemed like mutiny, but it was easy enough to convince them that the idea for the award had (alas) been mine, and that the ten thousand francs guaranteed by the phantom bank—of whose existence only the publisher could be sure—were for the moment a vague promise. Moreover, no one would have been pleased to have such a prestigious tribute go to a mentally retarded individual, no matter how talented she was. And so, in the end we made our decision in spite of the devil. Who did not take it very well: after a few days the burgomaster came down with pneumonia that almost sent him to the other world, and a week later councilor Linz was the victim of an automobile crash, which left him with his pelvis and both legs fractured. The cause of the accident? A fox had crossed the road in front of him.

I was spared. But for how much longer?

Already during those long hours devoted to the close scrutiny of the manuscripts, I would sometimes lose my concentration: while the words continued to flow, meaningless, before my eyes, my mind wandered elsewhere, on a parallel path, where unspeakable images flared up. They were thoughts that I had tried in every way to bury, thoughts that should never cross the mind of a God-fearing man, let alone a priest. Yet they were always present and left me no way out. They were flashes of pure hatred. The devil's pernicious influence continued to be felt even from a distance. I had to put an end to all this. But what weapons did I have to confront him with? A sprinkle of holy water would have less effect than a gob of spit in the eye—it certainly would not reduce him to ashes. He was not a spirit that could be driven off with prayer or exorcism; he was a physical, juridical entity and had to be dealt with as such.

14

When you want to avoid gruesome images, you resort to euphemism. To say that an army has suffered great losses is more acceptable than describing the horror of an appalling hecatomb. Liberating oneself of someone's presence generally means leaving him at the door, or avoiding spending time with him, but in a deeper sense it can mean wiping him off the face of the earth forever. So, when I say that the thought of freeing myself from the devil became increasingly obsessive, I mean that the desire to "do him in," literally, in the most sanguinary way, became ever stronger. I had already spotted a suitable weapon in the umbrella stand at the rectory, which held a nice bunch of sticks that the pastor would use for his sporadic walks. I had already chosen one that was good and sturdy, an Alpenstock with a solid brass handgrip. My adversary was a mortal being, after all, and even if he had the diabolical ability to be able to read other people's consciences, he was otherwise as vulnerable as we all are. Furthermore, the situation was changing. Now I could also count on a number of residents of

Dichtersruhe who silently harbored a grudge against that stranger who had treacherously entered their midst. In my most reckless fantasies I saw myself enter the café Oetker gripping my hiking stick as I headed directly to his table, striking him on the head with the full weight of the brass handle; I could even hear the sound of his skull bone shattering under my blows. But would I really go as far as that? Would I be able to face all the consequences of a murder? How would my parishioners react? Would they take my side? Would my act finally release them from the spell? All these questions gave me no respite. Yet I could see no other way out. If I let him live, it would not be long before he resumed his hold over the souls of Dichtersruhe.

Meanwhile, from the pulpit, I continued to accuse him of being an impostor whose sole intention was to con the villagers out of their money, leading them by the nose with the promise of a prize that would never be awarded. I even went so far as to declare with conviction that the man was the devil himself. And while earlier such a statement would have been met with an indulgent smile, now I saw their eyes widen in awareness. Many began to give credence to my statements. What I was saying had to be true, because never in the past had Dichtersruhe been torn apart by such profound hatred.

Meanwhile the devil acted like nothing was happening, and went on conducting his life as usual. He would arrive at café Oetker around ten in the morning to read the daily papers still fresh from the printer, then, around noon, he got ready to have a nice little lunch at someone else's expense. But things were changing. He no longer went to the Müllers' inn, ever since the owner had presented him with a bill that included arrears. Over time he'd run out of the Maria Mancini cigars, and the affectation of always carrying a manuscript in his pocket—which he would set beside him when he sat down at the table so he could read between mouthfuls, giving the appearance of a man totally dedicated to his work—no longer enthralled anyone. People kept their distance around him and no one was anxious to pay for his drinks at the bar anymore. My Sunday sermons were starting to bear fruit. By then few believed in the figure of the legendary publisher from Lucerne.

Then something happened that I interpreted as divine intervention. It was Marta Bauer, in fact, the unsuspecting rightful winner of the Goethe award, who gave him the coup de grâce, though knowing nothing about either him or his editorial chicanery.

During one of her rare strolls with her mother, the girl ran into the publisher as he was leaving the café Oetker. Usually she walked with her head down, avoiding any contact with strangers. But this time, as soon as young Marta saw him, she jerked her hand out of her mother's and ran toward him, barring his way.

"You're the devil, you're the devil ..." the girl began to chant, preventing him from continuing on. The scene was witnessed by several of the café's patrons who at that moment were sitting outdoors. At first Dr. Fuchs seemed to want to play along, awkwardly pretending to dodge young Marta, but she would not give up and stood before him with her arms outstretched, keeping him in his place. The scene indeed aroused the laughter of those present, but the game went on too long, and Dr. Fuchs lost his patience. "Get this stupid little monkey out of my way!" he shouted to the mother, who tried unsuccessfully to call her daughter back.

"This is utterly rude!" he exclaimed aloud, so that everyone could hear him, and thereupon he had no qualms about shoving the poor young girl aside; Marta, losing her balance, fell to the ground, hitting her head. Without making a move to help her, the elephant climbed over the monkey and proceeded on his way as if nothing had happened.

It turned out badly for him, however. Although the girl hadn't been hurt much, aside from a lump on her forehead, that show of irritation caused the devil to make enemies of half the village. Up till then he had lived by sponging off of others, but after that episode the creditors began knocking at his door, and the line kept growing longer: not only tradesmen and shopkeepers, but also simple craftsmen, painters, masons, and carpenters from whom he had commissioned a number of jobs to be done around the house. Now there was always someone waiting for him when he went out the door. And every so often a troop of rowdy kids crowded under his windows chanting hymns in praise of Beelzebub. Dr. Fuchs remained a prisoner—so to speak—in his apartments. He could only go out at night, because during the day a patrol of relentless creditors stood watch outside his door. Soon the small local bank denied him credit, demanding immediate repayment, and the Lions Club slammed the door in his face. Despite the fact that he was now on the ropes, the devil did not spare me a last menacing sign of his power: during my Sunday sermon, in which I once again discredited him, a rabid fox entered the church, arousing panic among the faithful. The animal passed through the central nave and vanished under the altar; even after the parishioners had left the church, the search turned out to be futile. No one was able to explain how the fox had entered and how he had gone out. It was certainly the devil's witchcraft. And this marked his end. People saw me as a kind of avenger, the only one who could liberate them. "Father Cornelius, deliver us from evil," they would say when they met me on the street. "Father, drive the devil out of our village. Make everything go back to the way it was before."

It was the local residents who asked me to do it. That's what I would tell the judge in my defense. I would also add that I should receive a commendation, not a sentence, for having eliminated the devil in person from the face of the earth. By now the requests from parishioners were becoming more persistent, until one day, as I was crossing the square, a young boy handed me a weapon, wrapped in an oilcloth, that would serve my purpose. The delivery of that macabre gift was so abrupt that I did not have time to find out who had sent it to me. Only later in the rectory did I unwrap it: it was a Swiss army regulation revolver. For me, having never touched a firearm in my life, that object had great allure. I spent hours gazing at the weapon, handling it with extreme caution, always fearful that it might explode in my hand. Only after having studied it meticulously did I dare open it. I took all the bullets out of the chamber and tried pulling the trigger. Even unloaded, the revolver filled me with uncontrollable fear; each time the hammer struck the firing pin, I felt my heart stop. I had to smile at the thought that the role of avenger had been assigned to me, of all people.

Days of hesitation passed. Finally I made up my mind. It's difficult to say why I chose to do it just that Sunday, just at that time of dusk, just when the shadow of the mountain was already darkening the square.

15

Although in my memory everything assumes fluctuat-
ing, volatile contours, I see myself crossing the distance
between the rectory and the devil's house with surprising
confidence, the loaded pistol in my pocket, determined to
put an end to it once and for all. I can measure every step,
every thought, every pounding heart beat. The lights of
his house are lit on the first floor. I know he's expecting
me. And in fact the door below opens gently when I nudge
it. My nerves are as taut as violin strings, my senses
magnified a hundredfold. Hovering in the rooms is a trace
of wormwood, of withered plants, rotten apples, burnt
wax, and stale smoke. I can distinguish every shift of
air—from the opening of the door to the page of a book
turning—, perceive every variation in temperature, every
lurch of my heartbeat, every dystonia, even the phenol
odor caused by fear.

Of all the rooms, one is lit by dozens of candles. I climb
the stairs, look in the doorway, and see his figure, standing, in shirt sleeves, with his loosened suspenders hanging down his sides like the handles of a bizarre piece of

gym equipment. Were it not for his body's abnormal girth, I would hardly recognize him without the black wig. But the voice is unmistakable.

"What a surprise, Reverend," he exclaims, pressing his hand to his breast in a feminine gesture, the grotesque replica of a primadonna caught in déshabillé in her dressing-room, "I wasn't really expecting an unannounced visit from you." He hurriedly slips on a roomy damask silk dressing gown, and to appear composed, lights one of his cigars. Then, following the direction of my gaze, he realizes that his skull is bare. He runs his fingers over his scalp with an idiotic smile.

"The wig? A requirement of the performance. By now no longer needed. The time for masquerades is over, isn't that so, my dear Cornelius? The play is about to end. To what do I owe your visit?"

"I came to say goodbye," I said. "Or rather, I bring farewells from the entire village." The tone of my voice was inflexible and solemn. I felt invested with an otherworldly mission.

The devil's only response was to pour some wine into a glass.

"Drink up, Cornelius, a toast then to our final parting."

Naturally, I was careful not to touch it, and after fumbling the revolver out of the pocket of my cassock, I waved it under his nose. Certainly there was nothing threatening about my gesture; I think that even to the eyes of a child it would have been obvious that I had no familiarity whatsoever with weapons. I was holding the revolver as if it were a boiled fish, and I nearly gripped it by the barrel. Perhaps it was the very inadequacy of my gesture that reassured him, to the degree that he sprawled in his armchair, inhaling deeply and savoring the smoke of one of his last Maria Mancinis.

"Did you at least switch off the safety?"

Until a moment ago I was certain that the revolver I was clenching had no such device … but now I began to have my doubts. Had the existence of some hidden mechanism escaped me? My expression of uncertainty did not go unnoticed. Was it so apparent then that I could not handle a firearm? Racheting up the pressure, the devil added:

"Did you oil the barrel well? You know that the least little foreign body is all it takes for it to explode in your hand. I know these contrivances and I can tell you that they are extremely dangerous. It is a weapon that has reaped more victims among those who aimed it than among those who were its target."

It occurred to me that in the bundle that was delivered to me, there was also a wooden case containing cylindrical pipe cleaners and brushes, which I hadn't even remotely thought of using, trusting that the intent of the person who had given me the revolver was to provide me with a weapon that for all practical purposes was ready to use, and not a rusty antique that I would have to clean.

"We'll find out when the time comes," I said, with not a hint of tremor in my voice as I loaded the barrel. I did so with determination. The very fact that there was a considerable chance that he would survive comforted me in a way, because I was partly shifting my responsibility to fate or to divine will. Though it was dictated by a kind of fatalism, my confidence seemed to throw him a curve.

Outside, voices could be heard; people were already gathering in the square.

"Do you hear them?" he said. "What can I be faulted for except the fact that I played along with their game? After all," the devil continued, "my work is nothing but a masterly job of maieutics: for each individual I try to draw out the worst that lies hidden in his soul. It is not always an easy task to awaken certain slumbering memories buried in the subconscious. Even you, my dear Cornelius, have a short memory apparently. Did you ever ask yourself why your parents wanted you to become a priest? Already in your first years of life they had discovered your true nature, and they were convinced that the cassock would protect you. But instead the evil came from within you; it was like an angry wasp that for some time had penetrated your armor. Evil was in your nature, you carried evil in you from the day you were born, and it already began to manifest itself in your early childhood. Do you remember when, during that school outing, you felt the irresistible urge to push your classmate off the trail that you were following in single file? He had leaned over a little too far to pick up a stone, and you couldn't resist giving him a little shove, just for laughs. No one was amused by your little joke, however, because your schoolmate was hurt very badly. And of course you remember Sammy, your beloved little dog whom you spent your days playing with. Until you got tired of his presence. You couldn't stand having him always underfoot anymore, so you got the idea of taking him into the woods and tying him to a tree with a little cord. Oh, of course, you don't remember that episode; to use an expression that is much in vogue today, you suppressed it. He managed to get free, Sammy did, and came back to you. But in what condition? And so you picked up that big rock from the ground. You could barely lift it up to your chest, remember?"

"That's not true," I said, "it's a bold-faced lie!"

But the devil went on undeterred.

"Later you spent a few years shut away within the walls of the seminary, where you taught philosophy. Until you met Stefan, that pale, ascetic young man. How did you describe him? *A young man who summed up all the qualities of those who are called to spiritual life.* He saw in you a teacher, a mentor, the one who would guide him in life, and who would dissolve his doubts, free him from all fear. A spiritual father, the father whom he had never known. He loved you as a son, but you certainly did not return his feelings with a corresponding paternal sentiment. Devoured by passion, which you mistook for love, you went beyond that, and when poor Stefan couldn't take the disillusionment, the revulsion, he threatened to take his own life. What better opportunity than that trip to the mountains to give him a little push and protect yourself from any possible accusations. But you didn't think about the fact that he might have a diary. Everything you told the police is false: Stefan did not get lost that night. He was right next to you, he was walking beside you, and when you passed the brink of that ravine, it was easy to give him a shove, just like you had done so many years ago, with your classmate. Naturally, you have suppressed all this. How can I blame you? Knowing that you are a potential killer is an intolerable weight, but what's even worse is to suspect it, to keep the floodgate closed at all times, so that the truth won't spill its banks and engulf your conscience."

I tried to answer, but in vain.

"Look at yourself, Reverend, the very fact that you are pointing that toy at me only confirms my theories. What I did not expect from you is that you would attack the parish priest as well. When you saw his letter in the mail, waiting to be sent to the bishop, you did not hesitate to open it and read its contents. Of course, it was I who planted the idea in the old man's head that he should send you away and have you confined for much-needed treatment, because you were already manifesting symptoms of madness. That way I would be rid of your irritating presence. The letter sent you into a rage, and you demanded clarifications from the pastor. And that same night, unable to sleep, you went to knock at his door: you knew you would find him still awake and hard at work, polishing his "memoirs of a country pastor," the title he intended to give the pages he'd labored over. Poor old man! To die a step away from seeing his dream come true. All you had to do was grab him by the collar and shake him like a rag doll to cause his heart to fail from stress."

"That's enough!" I shouted with as much breath as I had in me. I raised the barrel of the gun to his forehead. "One more word and I'll pull the trigger." But he remained unperturbed. He seemed to be amused by the idea of having uncovered the well whose depths revealed the drowsing snake's coils.

At that moment all my certainties began to waver. Even the weapon I clutched in my hand suddenly seemed quite inadequate to my adversary's elephantine girth. Expressions such as "body mass," "impact resistance," and "penetration force" kept echoing in my head, as if it were the end of an exhausting physics lesson. I was thinking about how effective that feeble pistol could be against his pachydermal bulk. Even assuming that the revolver didn't jam, I could miss the target on the first shot, giving him a chance to rush at me. That mass of fat suddenly seemed like an impenetrable barrier, able to stop any bullet. Nonetheless I realized that if I didn't do it at that moment, I would never do it. If I merely let him continue speaking, filling my head with more atrocious doubts, I would end up turning the weapon against myself.

So, I aimed high, at his forehead. Aiming is easy, it's like pointing an accusing finger at someone.

It seems impossible to perform an act and forget it the very instant it is done. To observe only its effects without being able to trace back to its causes, however recent they may be. That was what happened to me. Had it not been for the Parkinsonian tremor of my right hand, and for the muffled deafness in which my hearing seemed to float following the explosion, I would have said that nothing serious had happened, that the man with the abnormal body, resting in the armchair with his head thrown back, had simply fallen asleep, and that it would be best for me to leave on tiptoe so as not to wake him. And so I left the room and went down the stairs again. Only when I was about to leave did I realize that I was still holding the revolver. My first impulse was to run and toss it in the river, as if hiding it were an obligatory rule of the game, but since it was my firm intention to turn myself in, it seemed pointless to inconvenience an army of people willing and ready to search for material evidence. So before leaving, I decided to leave it in plain sight on a console in the vestibule.

Outside, the village seemed like a huge chaotic anthill: people swarmed from all directions, pouring into the main street and gathering in the middle of the square, where a gallows had been raised not far from Goethe's statue. It was surrounded on three sides by a pyramid of dried sticks, and at the top of the scaffold hung a puppet with the head of a pig. Someone poured a can of gasoline on the fagots and lit the fire. The flames rose high, and the cloth puppet, filled with straw and paper, burned quickly, leaving only the pig's head, which began to sizzle. Meanwhile people formed a line and stopped beside the pyre to feed it with whatever they were carrying: some tossed in a manuscript, others two or more, and as they did so, you could see an expression of beatitude on their faces before they moved on to make way for those who followed. Nothing sums up the torments and mysteries of literature like a burning page: the paper blackens and the words shine through in a paroxysmal flash before vanishing into the darkness from which they came. In the presence of that auto-da-fé, Goethe's gleaming bronze statue reflected the fiery tongues, and in the wavering glints of the flames, the poet's inspired face seemed to assume the most grotesque smirk of mockery, meant for the writers of Dichtersruhe.

Father Cornelius's story breaks off here. We can imagine a bus that completes its final night route to the end of the line. On board there is still one passenger who was supposed to get off earlier, but instead, lulled by the listless tedium of the engine, fell asleep for a long time, dreaming. The pneumatic puff of the doors woke him and he finds himself in an unknown suburb, at an unspecified hour of night, with no means of getting back.

This is the priest's state of mind at that moment, as Friedrich describes it to us: Father Cornelius sits there, motionless before him like one of Madame Tussaud's statues. He seems completely drained, unable to say a word. Until he also abruptly wakes up.

Father Cornelius seemed to awaken from a dream. And now he looked around, bewildered, as if he no longer recognized the place where he was. All at once he was jolted by an irresistible impulse that made him leap to his feet. Cautiously he approached the window. "Do you hear it?" he asked, shaking all over. His face expressed an unbearable torment. His agitation was transmitted to me.

"What?"

"The cry of the foxes."

"I don't hear anything," I said.

"Wherever I go, the foxes haunt me. Here too, and now they're announcing his coming."

I tried to reassure him. I went to the window to hear better, but outside a profound silence reigned. The priest meanwhile went over to a shelf where there were several bottles of liqueurs, made available for guests who might want a digestif at the end of the meal. He poured himself a glass of Kirsch and emptied it in one gulp; he poured another and another. Not satisfied, he took a long swig directly from the bottle. Noting that I was watching him, he gave me a forced smile.

"Thank you for having had the patience to listen to me," he said. "But now I'm tired, tomorrow morning I have to leave early."

He lingered awhile, standing there endlessly wringing his hands, his face ashen, clammy. Then, holding his wide-brimmed saturn under his arm, like a discus thrower at the end of a disappointing match, he climbed the stairs leading to the rooms above.

I don't know how much longer I stayed there, in that gloomy dining room. All I know is that when I got to my room, I dropped onto the bed feeling completely drained, without even the strength to undress. I lay there for hours staring at the exposed beams that made up the ceiling. Gazing at it fixedly, it began to sway, until it bent and twisted like a sheet of paper exposed to a flame, and the dark knots in the fir wood came to life. The knots were none other than the sharp faces and eyes of foxes. I can't say with certainty that I fell asleep, but for a few hours I definitely lost track of time. I don't know what called me back; maybe it was the confusion of voices coming from one of the other rooms on my floor. It was only later, around five a.m., that I clearly heard the sound of footsteps going down the stairs and the door below opening. The lamp on the bedside table had remained on. I approached the window, straining to hear. It was still pitch-black outside, but you could already sense dawn's arrival. And at that moment I too was able to hear the cry of the foxes. The sound coming from the forest was a chilling chorus, as if hell had been uncapped, letting out the wailing of the damned. It lasted for a few moments, then silence fell again.

The next morning I had to get up just when I was about to fall asleep. The prospect of returning to my uncle empty-handed put me in a very bad mood. Moreover, the evening spent listening to the priest until the wee hours had left me completely nonplussed. I felt unfortunate, robbed, defrauded. In an instant I had been deprived of a harvest of dreams, future hopes, and ambitions. The story I had listened to weighed on my aspirations like a tombstone. Moreover, the weather was changing for the worse and already the asphalt on the road had darkened under an insistent drizzle. I skipped breakfast and ordered only coffee; I didn't feel like eating anything. I still had a good half hour before the arrival of the bus that would take me to the train station in Zurich. I went back to my room to finish packing my suitcase, but the waitress—the same one who had served us dinner the evening before—stopped me in the corridor to ask if I knew Father Cornelius's address by any chance. It seemed that in his haste to leave, the priest had left some of his personal things behind, and she didn't know where to send them to him. I glanced into the room and saw his cassock hanging on a coat stand, topped by his saturn tilted at a jaunty angle.

Only a few weeks after my return, I read this news item in a Zurich newspaper:

In the vicinity of Küsnacht, a forest ranger discovered the body of a man at the bottom of a cliff, already in a state of decomposition. It was not possible to immediately verify his identity with any certainty, because his face was completely mangled by foxes. However, from the documents in his possession, it appears that he was Professor Cornelius G.—at one time an esteemed lecturer and psychotherapist. In academic circles he was known by his colleagues for his farfetched theories, as well as for his eccentric ways (although he had abandoned the priesthood, the professor had never given up wearing the cassock). In 1981 his name had appeared in the annals of the crime pages when he was accused and tried for the brutal assassination of a German publisher, who was spending his vacation in Switzerland at the time. The accused is said to have maintained his innocence before the judge, with a single sentence: "That was the devil in person, and you should all be grateful to me for having rid the world of his nefarious presence." Recognizing his diminished capacity, the judge ordered him to be interned in a psychiatric hospital where, until a year ago, he'd undergone treatment for over nine years before being released; he was said to be completely cured, according to experts who had observed him, and therefore able to resume his activities as educator and lecturer.

For several months after my return from Küsnacht, I was visited nearly every night by the recurrent nightmare of foxes
besieging me. Only toward the end of winter did those fright-
ful dreams become less frequent, before ceasing altogether
at the beginning of spring.

With these words the story narrated by Friedrich, or whatever his name is, concludes.

For a long time I asked myself what to do with this text.
I was the depositary entrusted with it, but without any
instructions regarding its disposition. I had not written
it, so I did not feel authorized to publish it. Moreover, the
anonymous author claimed to have heard the story from
an unknown stranger. All this left me facing a problem
whose solution was thorny. Who is actually the legitimate
owner of a "manuscript found in a bottle"? The one who
relinquished it to the currents of the sea, or the individual who found it at the water's edge? And if the author
chose to remain anonymous, can he still claim the rights
to what he wrote? Can his having sent it to me be interpreted as an implicit request to publish it? If not that, why
else?

TRANSLATOR'S NOTE:

A saturn is a cleric's hat with a wide, circular brim and a rounded crown, worn along with the cassock when outdoors. Egregore (also egregor) expresses a psychic concept that may be thought of as a "collective group mind," which influences the thinking of a group of people. The Föhn is a warm, dry wind that descends a mountain, e.g. on the north side of the Alps. The term *le diable boiteux*, literally, the lame devil, may allude to a 1707 novel by French writer Alain-René Lesage called *Le Diable boiteux*; a 1948 French film of the same name (*The Lame Devil* in the US, *The Devil Who Limped* in the UK) is a biography of French diplomat Talleyrand, to whom that nickname was applied. Jass is a card game played by taking tricks, supposedly the precursor of pinochle. The Maria Mancini cigars recall Thomas Mann's *The Magic Mountain* (1924), whose main character, Hans Castrop, habitually enjoys a cigar of that brand. The aphorism attributed to Goethe, *art is long, life is short, judgment difficult*, reprises Hippocrates' *ars longa, vita brevis, occasio praeceps, experimentum periculosum, iudicium difficile.*

On the Design

As book design is an integral part of the reading experience, we would like to acknowledge the work of those who shaped the form in which the story is housed.

Tessa van der Waals (Netherlands) is responsible for the cover design, cover typography and art direction of all World Editions books. She works in the internationally renowned tradition of Dutch Design. Her bright and powerful visual aesthetic maintains a harmony between image and typography and captures the unique atmosphere of each book. She works closely with internationally celebrated photographers, artists, and letter designers. Her work has frequently been awarded prizes for Best Dutch Book Design.

The cover image was taken by photographer Charles Fréger (France), whose images of 'tribal Europe' were captured over two winters of travel, through 19 countries. The transformation of humans into beasts is a central aspect of centuries-old pagan rituals that celebrate the changing seasons, fertility, and life and death. The costumes vary between regions and even between villages; they often represent devils, goats, wild boars, bears, or death itself. The character on the front is known as Habergeiss.

The cover has been edited by lithographer Bert van der Horst of BFC Graphics (Netherlands).

Suzan Beijer (Netherlands) is responsible for the typography and careful interior book design of all World Editions titles.

The text on the inside covers and the press quotes are set in Circular, designed by Laurenz Brunner (Switzerland) and published by Swiss type foundry Lineto.

All World Editions books are set in the typeface Dolly, specifically designed for book typography. Dolly creates a warm page image perfect for an enjoyable reading experience. This typeface is designed by Underware, a European collective formed by Bas Jacobs (Netherlands), Akiem Helmling (Germany), and Sami Kortemäki (Finland). Underware are also the creators of the World Editions logo, which meets the design requirement that 'a strong shape can always be drawn with a toe in the sand.'